Blaze

Dear Reader,

After my Harlequin Blaze title *One Wild Wedding Night* was released in January of 2008, I heard from a lot of readers. Most of them especially enjoyed Tony and Gloria's story—the last one in the collection—about a married couple trying to recapture the sizzle by playing a little game of strangers-in-a-bar.

The idea of playing sexy games is definitely an exciting one. Years ago, I was one of those readers who snapped up *101 Nights of Grrreat Sex*, the book where you tore open an envelope that suggested an entire sensual scenario for you and your partner (the things we do for research). And the concept of keeping things fresh by enacting role-playing fantasies never left my mind.

So when I got the chance to contribute to the popular Forbidden Fantasies miniseries in the Blaze imprint, I wanted to do the theme justice. Having a secret affair and indulging in lots of sexy, role-playing games sounded both forbidden...and extremely sexy. Blazingly so, in fact.

I love hearing from readers. If you would like to let me know what you think of *Play with Me*, please drop me a line through my Web site, www.lesliekelly.com, or visit me on my blog, www.plotmonkeys.com.

Thanks and happy reading!

Leslie Kelly

Leslie Kelly

PLAY WITH ME

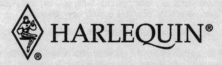

TORONTO • NEW YORK • LONDON
AMSTERDAM • PARIS • SYDNEY • HAMBURG
STOCKHOLM • ATHENS • TOKYO • MILAN • MADRID
PRAGUE • WARSAW • BUDAPEST • AUCKLAND

Recycling programs
for this product may
not exist in your area.

ISBN-13: 978-0-373-79525-3

PLAY WITH ME

Copyright © 2010 by Leslie A. Kelly.

This edition published by arrangement with Harlequin Books S.A.

® and TM are trademarks of the publisher. Trademarks indicated with ® are registered in the United States Patent and Trademark Office, the Canadian Trade Marks Office and in other countries.

www.eHarlequin.com

Printed in U.S.A.

ABOUT THE AUTHOR

Leslie Kelly has written more than two dozen books and novellas for Harlequin Blaze, Harlequin Temptation and HQN Books. Known for her sparkling dialogue, fun characters and depth of emotion, her books have been honored with numerous awards, including a National Readers' Choice Award, and three nominations for the RWA RITA® Award.

Leslie resides in Maryland with her own romantic hero, Bruce, and their three daughters. Visit her online at www.lesliekelly.com.

Books by Leslie Kelly

HARLEQUIN BLAZE
347—OVEREXPOSED
369—ONE WILD WEDDING NIGHT
402—SLOW HANDS
408—HEATED RUSH
447—BLAZING BEDTIME STORIES
    "My, What a Big…You Have!"

To loyal romance readers everywhere.

In this economy, I know it's got to be really tough to indulge your reading habits. I sincerely appreciate each and every one of you who keeps buying books so that I can keep writing them.

Thank you so much.

Prologue

Columbus Day

"Do you know what your problem is?"

Reese Campbell didn't even look up as the door to his office burst open and the familiar voice of his extremely nosy, bossy great-aunt intruded on what had been a relatively quiet October morning. Because that was one hell of a loaded question.

Hmm. Problem? What problem? Did he have a *problem?*

Being thrust into a job he hadn't been ready for, hadn't planned on, hadn't even wanted? That was kind of a problem.

Being thrust into that job because his father had died unexpectedly, at the age of fifty-five? Aside from being an utter tragedy, that was absolutely a problem.

Battling competitors who'd figured him to be a pushover when he'd stepped in to run a large brewery while only in his mid-twenties? Problem.

Dealing with longtime employees who didn't like the changes he was implementing in the family business? Problem.

Ending a relationship because the woman didn't appreciate that he—a good-time guy—now had so many responsibilities? Problem.

Walking a tightrope with family members who went from begging him to keep everything the way it was, to resenting his every effort to fill his father's shoes? Big effing problem.

"Did you hear me?"

He finally gave his full attention to his great-aunt Jean, who had never seen a closed door she hadn't wanted to fling wide open. He had to smile as he beheld her red hat and flashy sequined jacket. Going into old age gracefully had never entered his aunt's mind. Keeping her opinions to herself hadn't, either.

"I heard," he replied.

"Well, do you know?"

What he didn't know was why she was asking. Because she didn't *want* an answer. Rhetorical questions like that one were always the opening volley in the elderly woman's none-of-your-damn-business assaults on everyone else's private life.

He leaned back in his chair. "Whatever it is, I am quite sure you're about to tell me."

"Cheeky," she said, closing the door. "You're bored."

No kidding.

"You're twenty-nine years old and you're suffocating. For two years, you haven't drawn one free, unencumbered breath."

He remained still, silent. Wary. Because so far, his eccentric, opinionated great-aunt was absolutely, one hundred percent correct.

Suffocating. That was a good word to describe his life these days. An appropriate adjective for the frequent sensation that an unbearable weight had landed on his chest and was holding him in place, unable to move.

As Aunt Jean said, his breath had been stolen, his momentum stopped. All forward thought frozen in place, glued to that moment in time when a slick road and a blind curve had changed everything he and his family had known about their former lives.

"You need some excitement. An adventure. How long has it been since you've had sex?"

Reese coughed into his fist, the mouthful of air he'd just inhaled having lodged in his throat. "Aunt Jean…"

She grunted. "Oh, please, spare me. You need to get laid."

"Jeez, can't you bake or knit or something like a normal great-aunt?"

She ignored him. "Have you gotten any since that stupid Tate girl tried to get you to choose her over your family?" Not waiting for an answer, she continued. "You've got to do something more than deal with your sad mother, your squabbling sisters and your juvenile-delinquent brother."

He stiffened, the reaction a reflexive one.

"Oh, don't get indignant, you know it's true," she said. "I love them as much as you do, we're family. But even apples from the same tree sometimes harbor an occasional worm."

The woman did love her metaphors.

"So here's what you do."

"I knew you would get around to telling me eventually."

She ignored him. "You simply must have an adventure."

"Okay, got it. One adventure, coming right up," he said with a deliberate eye roll. "Should I call 1-800-Wild Times or just go to letsgetcrazy.com?"

"You're not so old I can't box your ears."

A grin tugged at his mouth. "The one time you boxed my ears as a kid, I put frogs in your punch bowl right before a party."

An amused gleam lit her eyes. "So do it again."

Reese's brow furrowed. "Excuse me?"

"Be wild. Do something fun. Chuck this cautious-businessman gig and be the bad-ass rebel you once were."

Bad-ass rebel? Him? The guy most recently voted Young Businessman of the Year? "Yeah, right."

He didn't know which sounded more strange—him being that person, or his elderly great-aunt using the term bad-ass rebel. Then again, she *had* just asked him when he'd last gotten laid—a question he didn't even want to contemplate in his own mind.

She fixed a pointed stare at his face. "Don't think I've forgotten who I had to bail out of jail one spring break. Which young fellow it was who ended up taking two girls to the prom. Or who hired a stripper to show up at the principal's house."

Oh. That bad-ass rebel. Reese had forgotten all about him.

"The world was your playground once. Go play in it again."

Play? Be unencumbered, free from responsibilities?

Reese looked at the files on his desk. There was a mountain of order forms, requisitions, payroll checks, ad copy, legal paperwork—all needing his attention. His signature. His time.

Then there was his personal calendar, filled with family obligations, fixing his sister's car, talking to his brother's coach...doing father stuff that he hadn't envisioned undertaking for another decade at least.

All his responsibility. Not in a decade. Now.

It wasn't the life he'd envisioned for himself. But it *was* the life he had. And there wasn't a thing he could do about it.

"I've forgotten how," he muttered.

She didn't say anything for a long moment, then the elderly woman, whose energy level so belied her years, laughed softly. There was a note in that laugh, both secretive and sneaky.

"Whatever it is you're thinking about doing, forget it."

She feigned a look of hurt. "Me? What could I possibly do?"

He knew better than to be fooled by the nice-old-lady routine. She'd been playing that card for as long as he could remember and it had been the downfall of many a more gullible family member. "I'm going to leave a note that if I am kidnapped by a troupe of circus clowns, the police should talk to you."

She tsked. "Oh, my boy, circus clowns? Is that the best you can come up with? I'm wounded—you've underestimated me."

"Aunt Jean..."

Ignoring him, she turned toward the door. Before she exited, however, she glanced back. "I have the utmost confidence in you, dear. I have no doubt that when the right moment presents itself, you will rise to the occasion."

With a quickly blown kiss and a jangle of expensive

bracelets decorating her skinny arm, she slipped out. Reese was free to get back to work. But instead, he spent a few minutes thinking about what Great-Aunt Jean had said.

He didn't doubt she was right about the fact that he was bored. Stifled. Suffocating. But her solution—to go a little crazy—wasn't the answer. Not for the life he was living now. Not when so many people counted on him. His family. His employees. His late father.

Besides, it didn't matter. No opportunity to play, as she put it, had come his way for a long time. Not in more than two years. The word wasn't even in his vocabulary anymore.

And frankly, Reese didn't see that changing anytime soon.

1

Halloween

IT SHOULD HAVE BEEN a routine flight.

Pittsburgh to Chicago was about as simple an itinerary as Clear-Blue Airlines ever flew. In the LearJet 60, travel time would be under an hour. The weather was perfect, the sky like something out of a kid's Crayola artwork display. Blue as a robin's egg, with a few puffy white clouds to set the scene and not a drop of moisture in the air. Crisp, not cold, it was about the most beautiful autumn day they'd had this year.

The guys in the tower were cheerful, the Lear impeccably maintained and a joy to handle. Amanda Bauer's mood was good, especially since it was one of her favorite holidays. Halloween.

She should have known something was going to screw it up.

"What do you mean Mrs. Rush canceled?" she asked, frowning as she held the cell phone tightly to her ear. Standing in the shadow of the jet on the tarmac, she edged in beside the fold-down steps. She covered her other ear with her hand to drown out the noises of nearby aircraft. "Are you sure? She's been talking about this trip for ages."

"Sorry, kiddo, you're going to have to do without your senior sisters meeting this month," said Ginny Tate, the backbone of Clear-Blue. The middle-aged woman did everything from scheduling appointments, to book-keeping, to ordering parts, to maintaining the company Web site. Ginny was just as good at arguing with airport honchos who wanted to obsess over every flight plan as she was at making sure Uncle Frank, who had founded the airline, took his cholesterol medication every day.

In short, Ginny was the one who kept the business running so all Amanda and Uncle Frank—now 60-40 partners in the airline—had to do was fly.

Which was just fine with them.

"Mrs. Rush said one of her friends has the flu and she doesn't want to go away in case she comes down with it, too."

"Oh, that bites," Amanda muttered, really regretting the news. Because she had been looking forward to see-ing the group of zany older women again. Mrs. Rush, an elderly widow and heir to a steel fortune, was one of her regular clients.

The wealthy woman and her "gal pals," who ranged in age from fifty to eighty, took girls-weekend trips every couple of months. They always requested Amanda as their pilot, having almost adopted her into the group. She'd flown them to Vegas for some gambling. To Reno for some gambling. To the Caribbean for some gambling. With a few spa destinations thrown in between.

Amanda had no idea what the group had planned for Halloween in Chicago, but she was sure it would have been entertaining.

"She asked me to tell you she's sorry, and says if she has to, she'll invent a trip in a few weeks so you two can catch up."

"You do realize she's not kidding."

"I know," said Ginny. "Money doesn't stand a chance in her wallet, does it? The hundred-dollar bills have springs attached—she puts them in and they start trying to bounce right out."

Pretty accurate. Since losing her husband, the woman had made it her mission to go through as much of his fortune as possible. Mr. Rush hadn't lived long enough to enjoy the full fruits of his labors, so in his memory, his widow was going to pluck every plum and wring every bit of juice she could out of the rest of her life. No regrets, that was her M.O.

Mrs. Rush was about as different from the people Amanda had grown up with as a person could be. Her own family back in Stubing, Ohio, epitomized the small-town, hard-work, wholesome, nose-to-the-grindstone-'til-the-day-you-die mentality.

They had never quite known what to make of *her*.

Amanda had started rebelling by first grade, when she'd led a student revolt against lima beans in school lunches. Things had only gone downhill from there. By the time she hit seventh grade, her parents were looking into boarding schools…which they couldn't possibly afford. And when she graduated high school with a disciplinary record matched only by a guy who'd ended up in prison, they'd pretty much given up on her for good.

She couldn't say why she'd gone out of her way to find trouble. Maybe it was because *trouble* was such a bad word in her house. The forbidden path was always so much more exciting than the straight-and-narrow one.

There was only one member of the Bauer clan who was at all like her: Uncle Frank. His motto was *Live 'til your fuel tank is in the red and then keep on going. You can rest during your long dirt nap when you finally slide off the runway of life.*

Live to the extreme, take chances, go places, don't wait for anything you want, go out and find it or make it happen. And never let anyone tie you down.

These were all lessons Amanda had taken to heart when growing up, hearing tales of her wild uncle Frank, her father's brother, of whom everyone else in the family had so disapproved. They especially disliked that he seemed to have his own personal parking space in front of the nearest wedding chapel. He'd walked down the aisle four times.

Unfortunately, he'd also walked down the aisle of a divorce courtroom just as often.

He might not be lucky in love, but he was as loyal an uncle as had ever been born. Amanda had shown up on his Chicago doorstep three days after her high school graduation and never looked back. Nor had her parents ever hinted they wanted her to.

He'd welcomed her, adjusted his playboy lifestyle for her—though he needn't have. Her father might hate his brother's wild ways, but Amanda didn't give a damn who he slept with.

From day one, he had assumed a somewhat-parental role and harassed her into going to college. He'd made sure she went home for obligatory visits to see the folks. But he'd also shown her the world. Opened her eyes so wide, she hadn't wanted to close them even to sleep in those early days.

He'd given her the sky…and he'd given her wings to

explore it by teaching her to fly. Eventually, he'd taken her in as a partner in his small regional charter airline and together they'd tripled its size and quadrupled its revenues.

Their success had come at a cost, of course. Neither of them had much of a social life. Even ladies' man Uncle Frank had been pretty much all-work-and-no-play since they'd expanded their territory up and down the east coast two years ago.

As for Amanda, aside from having a vivid fantasy life, when she wasn't in flight, she was as boring as a single twenty-nine-year-old could be. Evidence of that was her disappointment at not getting to spend a day with a group of old ladies who bitched about everything from their lazy kids to the hair growing out of their husbands' ears. Well, except Mrs. Rush, who sharply reminded her friends to be thankful for their husbands' ear hair while they still had husbandly ear hair to be thankful for.

"Well, so much for a fun Halloween," she said with a sigh.

"Honey, if sitting in a plane listening to a bunch of rich old ladies kvetch about their latest collagen injections is the only thing you've got to look forward to…"

"I know, I know." It did sound pathetic. And one of these days, she really needed to do something about that. Get working on a real social life again, rather than throwing herself into her job fourteen hours a day, and spending the other ten thinking about all the things she would do if she had the time.

Picturing those things, even.

She closed her eyes, willing that thought away. Her

fantasy life might be a rich and vivid one. But it was definitely not suitable for work hours.

Problem was, ever since she'd realized just how dangerous she was to men's hearts, she really hadn't felt like going after their bodies.

Her last relationship had ended badly. Very badly. And she still hadn't quite gotten over the regret of it.

"What a shame. Mrs. Rush would have loved your costume."

"Oh, God, don't remind me," Amanda said with a groan.

It was for the benefit of the ladies that she'd worn it. Mrs. Rush had ordered her to let loose on this one holiday trip.

Gulping, Amanda glanced around, hoping nobody was close enough to see her getup. She needed to dart up into the plane and change because while the old-fashioned outfit would have made her passengers cackle with glee, she didn't particularly want to be seen by any of the workers or baggage handlers on the tarmac. Not to mention the fact that, even though the weather was great, it *was* October and she was freezing her butt off.

The Clear-Blue uniform she usually wore was tailored and businesslike, no-nonsense. Navy blue pants, crisp white blouse, meant to inspire confidence and get the customer to forget their pilot was only in her late twenties. Most customers liked that. However, the older women in the senior-gal group always harassed Amanda about her fashion sense. They insisted she would be one hot tamale if she'd lose the man-clothes and get girly.

She glanced down at herself again and had to smile. You couldn't get much more girly than this ancient stewardess costume, complete with white patent-leather go-go boots and hot pants that clung to her butt and skimmed the tops of her thighs.

She looked like she'd stepped out of a 1972 commercial for Southwest Airlines.

As costumes went, it wasn't bad, if she did say so herself. Shopping for vintage clothes on e-bay, she'd truly lucked out. The psychedelic blouse was a bit tight, even though she wasn't especially blessed in the boob department, and she couldn't button the polyester vest that went over it. But the satiny short-shorts fit perfectly, and the boots were so kick-ass she knew she would have to wear them again without the costume.

"Now, before you go worrying that your day is a total wash," Ginny said, sounding businesslike again, "I wanted to let you know that the trip was not in vain. I've got you a paying passenger back to Chicago who'll make it worth your while."

"Seriously? A sudden passenger from Pittsburgh, on a Saturday?" she asked. This wasn't exactly a hotbed destination like Orlando or Hartsfield International. Mrs. Rush was the only customer they picked up regularly in this part of Pennsylvania and most business types didn't charter flights on weekends.

"Yes. When Mrs. Rush called to cancel, she told me a local businessman needed a last-minute ride to Chicago. She put him in touch with us, hoping you could help him. I told him you were there and would have no problem bringing him back with you."

Perfect. A paying gig, and she could make it home in time to attend her best friend Jazz's annual Halloween party.

Then she reconsidered. Honestly, it was far more likely she would end up staying home, devouring a bag of Dots and Tootsie Rolls while watching old horror films on AMC. Because Jazz—Jocelyn Wilkes, their lead mechanic at Clear-Blue and the closest friend Amanda had ever had—was a wild one whose parties always got crashed and sometimes got raided. Amanda just wasn't in the mood for a big, wild house party with a ton of strangers.

Being honest, she'd much prefer a small, wild bed-room one—with only two guests. It was just too bad for her that, lately, the only guest in her bedroom had come with batteries and a scarily illustrated instruction manual written in Korean.

"Manda? Everything okay?"

"Absolutely," she said, shaking the crazy thoughts out of her head. "Glad I get to earn my keep today."

Ginny laughed softly into the phone. "You earn your keep every day, kiddo. I don't know what Frank would do without you."

"The feeling is most definitely mutual."

She meant that. Amanda hated to even think of what her life might be like if she hadn't escaped the small, closed-in, claustrophobic world she'd lived in with the family who had so disapproved of her and tried so hard to change her.

She had about as much in common with her cold, repressed parents and her completely subservient sister as she did with…well, with the swinging 1970s flower-power stewardess who'd probably once worn this uni-form. When she'd stood in line to get doused in the gene pool, she'd gotten far more of her uncle Frank's reckless, free-wheeling, never-can-stand-to-be-tied-down genes than her parents' staid, conservative ones.

She had several exes who would testify to that. One

still drunk-dialed her occasionally just to remind her she'd broken his heart. *Yeah. Thanks. Good to know.*

Even that, though, was better than thinking about the last guy she'd gotten involved with. He'd fallen in love. She'd fallen in "this is better than sleeping alone." Upon figuring that out, he'd tried to *make* her feel something more by staging a bogus overdose. She'd been terrified, stricken with guilt—and then, when he'd admitted what he'd done and *why,* absolutely furious rather than sympathetic.

Making things worse, he'd had the nerve to paint her as the bad guy. Her ears still rang with his accusations about just what a cold, heartless bitch she was.

Better cold and heartless than a lying, manipulative psycho. But it was also better to stay alone than to risk getting tangled up with another one.

So her Korean vibrator it was.

Some people were meant for commitment, family, all that stuff. Some, like her uncle Frank, weren't. Amanda was just like him; everybody said so. Including Uncle Frank.

"You'd better go. Your passenger should be there soon."

"Yeah. I definitely need to change my clothes before some groovy, foxy guy asks me if I want to go get high and make love not war at the peace rally," Amanda replied.

"Please don't on my account."

That hadn't come from Ginny.

Amanda froze, the phone against her face. It took a second to process, but her brain finally caught up with her ears and she realized she had indeed heard a strange voice.

It had been male. Deep, husky. And close.

"I gotta go," she muttered into the phone, sliding it closed before Ginny could respond.

Then she shifted her eyes, spying a pair of men's shoes not two feet from where she stood in the shadow of the Lear. Inside those shoes was a man wearing dark gray pants. Wearing them nicely, she had to acknowledge when she lifted her gaze and saw the long legs, the lean hips, the flat stomach.

Damn, he was well-made. Her throat tightened, her mouth going dry. She forced herself to swallow and kept on looking.

White dress shirt, unbuttoned at the strong throat. Thick arms flexing against the fabric that confined them. Broad shoulders, one of which was draped with a slung-over suit jacket that hung loosely from his masculine fingers.

Then the face. Oh, what a face. Square-jawed, hollow-cheeked. His brow was high, his golden-brown hair blown back by the light autumn breeze tunneling beneath the plane. And he had an unbelievably great mouth curved into a smile. A wide one that hinted at unspilled laughter lurking behind those sensual lips. She suspected that behind his dark sunglasses, his eyes were laughing, too.

Laughing at *her*.

Wonderful. One of the most handsome men she had ever seen in her entire life had just heard her muttering about groovy dudes and free love. All while she looked like Marcia Brady before a big cheerleading tryout.

"Guess I should have worn my bell-bottoms and tie-dyed, peace-sign shirt," he said.

She feigned a disapproving frown. "Your hair's much

too short, and not nearly stringy enough." Tsking, she added, "And no mustache?"

The sexy smile was companion to a sexy laugh. Double trouble, either way you sliced it. "I hate to admit it, but I'm not a Bob Dylan fan, either. I guess I really can't turn on, tune in and drop out."

"What a drag! If you say you can't play 'Blowin' in the Wind' on the guitar, I'm afraid I'm going to have to shove you into the engines of that 747 over there."

He held both hands up, palms out. "Peace! I really do dig the threads, sister," he said. "They're pretty groovalicious."

"Ooh, how very Austin Powers of you."

Wincing as if she'd hit him, he muttered, "Do chicks really go for dudes with bear pelts on their chests?"

"Not this one," she admitted with a laugh, liking this stranger already, despite her initial embarrassment. "Obviously, if you own a calendar, you know today's Halloween."

"Yeah, I heard that somewhere. That could explain why I passed a group of Hannah Montanas and Sponge-Bobs walking down the street on my way here."

"I don't know whether to be more sad that kids have to trick-or-treat in the daytime, or that you know who Hannah Montana and SpongeBob are."

"Nieces and nephews," he explained.

The affectionate way he said the words made her suspect he liked kids, which usually indicated a good nature. One point for the hot guy.

Correction, one *more* point for the hot guy. He'd already scored about a million for being so damned hot.

She also noted that he'd said nieces and nephews... not kids of his own. *Single?*

He glanced around at the other small planes nearby, and the few airport employees scurrying around doing the luggage-shuffle waltz. "So, nobody else got the invite to the costume party?"

Just her. Wasn't she the lucky one? "I was supposed to be picking up a regular passenger and she made me promise to dress up. This is definitely not my usual workplace attire."

"Rats. Here I was thinking I'd suddenly been let in the super-secret club. The *true* reason charter flights are so popular. You're saying it really *is* just to miss the long lines at security, and have some travel flexibility? It's not the hot pants and go-go boots?"

She shook her head. "'Fraid not. But don't forget, you also get to drink more than a half-cup of warm Coke and eat more than four pretzels."

"Well, okay then, we're on."

Amanda suddenly sighed, acknowledging what she'd managed to overlook. For just a minute or two, she had been able to convince herself that some sexy, passing stranger had noticed her and come over.

Passing by on a private, secured tarmac? Don't think so.

He wasn't some random passerby, she just knew it.

"Oh, hell. You're my passenger."

"If you're headed for Chicago, I think I am." He stuck out his hand. "Reese Campbell."

Cursing Mrs. Rush and Halloween and that stupid vintage clothing store on eBay, she put her hand in his. "Amanda Bauer."

Their first touch brought a flush of warmth, a flash of pleasure that was unexpected and a little surprising. The handshake lasted a second too long, was perhaps a hint more than a casual greeting among strangers. And while the exchange was entirely appropriate, she suddenly found herself thinking of all the touches she hadn't had for so long, all the *in*appropriate ways that strong, masculine hand could slide over her body.

Instant lust. It was real. Who knew?

She stared at him, trying to see the eyes behind the sunglasses, wondering if they had darkened with immediate interest the way hers probably had. Wondering what she might do about it if he returned that interest.

Get a grip.

Amanda regretfully tugged her hand away, pushing it down to her side and sliding it over her satin-covered hip. Her fingertips quivered as they brushed against the bare skin of her upper thigh and she suspected her palms were damp.

Forcing herself to take a deep, calming breath, she managed a smile. "Well, thanks for choosing Clear-Blue Air. We…"

"Love to fly, and it shows?"

It took her a second, then she placed the old Delta slogan. Her smile faded. The guy was way too hot to also be quick-witted and flirtatious. She could handle one at a time—it just became a little more distracting when they were all wrapped up in one extremely sexy package.

You can handle him. No sweat. Just stay professional.

Professional. While she was dressed for a love-in with the local beatnik crowd and this guy was both gorgeous and freaking adorable. *Right.*

"It'll be a quick trip," she said, gesturing toward the

steps and moving back so he could ascend them ahead of her.

No way was she going in first, not with the length of the damn hot pants. Her cheeks were pretty well covered as long as she remained still. If she walked up the steps with him behind her, however, all bets would be off. He'd get an eyeful, and it wouldn't be of London, *or* France. Because the stupid shorts were too form-fitting to wear even the most skimpy of underpants, unless they were ass-flossers, which she didn't even own.

"Wait," he said, pausing on the bottom step. "Aren't you going to say 'Fly me' or at least 'Welcome aboard'?"

She didn't. The softly muttered word that came out of her mouth was a lot less welcoming. And had fewer letters—four to be precise.

He shook his head and tsked. "Not exactly the friendly skies. Haven't caught the spirit yet this morning?"

"Make one more airline slogan crack and you'll be walking to Chicago," she said.

He nodded once, then pushed his sunglasses up onto the top of his tousled hair. The move revealed blue eyes that matched the sky above. And yeah. They were twinkling. Damn it.

"Understood. Just, uh, promise me you'll say 'Coffee, tea, or me' at least once, okay? Please?"

Amanda tried to glare, but that twinkle sucked the annoyance right out of her. Something irrepressible deep inside made her smirk and order, "Stop flirting. Start traveling."

He immediately got the vague Southwest Airlines reference. "Gotcha." With a grin, he added, "I'm starting to suspect I'm going to experience something pretty special in the air."

She groaned. "You do realize you're a total nerd for knowing all these old slogans."

The insult bounced right off him. "Nerd, huh?" Then he threw his head back and laughed. Innate good humor flowed off this sexy man who, though dressed like a businessman, wasn't like anyone she'd ever shuttled before. "Something tells me this is going to be a trip I won't soon forget," he said, something warm and knowing appearing in those deep blue eyes.

She could only draw in a slow breath as he climbed into the plane, thinking about that laughter and that twinkle, wondering why both of them made her insides all soft. As she watched her passenger disappear into the small jet, she also had to wonder about the trip she was about to take.

Coffee and tea they had, and he was welcome to them. But her? Well, she'd never even considered making a move on a customer before. Talk about unprofessional. Even the original hound dog himself Uncle Frank would kill her. He swore he never mixed business with pleasure.

And yet, how often was it that she actually met someone new, someone sexy and funny and entertaining? Considering her moratorium on anything that resembled dating, maybe a one-night stand with somebody from out of town, somebody she would never see again, was the perfect way to go.

Something inside her suddenly wanted to take a chance, to be a little outrageous. Maybe it was the playful, dangerous holiday—she'd always loved Halloween. It could have been the fortuitous change in passengers from wild old ladies to supremely sexy young man. Maybe it was the costume. The damned hot pants were hugging her open-and-alert-and-ready-for-business sex, the seam doing indecent things to her suddenly throbbing girl bits.

How long since she had done indecent things—or decent ones, for that matter—with a sexy man? Not since before they'd thrown all their energies into expanding Clear-Blue Air, at least. She hadn't had time for a lunch date, much less anything like the lust-fests she'd enjoyed in her younger years. The kind that lasted for entire weekends and involved not leaving a bed except to grab some sort of sensuous food that could be smeared onto—and eaten off of—someone else's hot, naked, sweat-tinged body.

She closed her eyes, her hand clenching tight on the railing. Her heart fluttered in her chest and she tried to make herself move. But she couldn't—not climbing up, but not backing away, either. Not physically, and not in her head.

Was she really considering this? God, she hadn't even looked at Reese Campbell's left hand to make sure he was available. She had no idea if he was actually attracted to her or just an irrepressible flirt. Yet something inside was telling her to take a shot with this complete stranger.

It was crazy, something she'd never considered. Yet right now, at this moment, she was definitely considering it. If he was available…could she do it? Seduce a stranger? Have an anonymous fling with a random man, like something out of a blue movie on late-night cable?

She didn't know, but it sounded good. Given the

current craziness of her life—her work schedule, travel, commitment to her uncle and his company, plus her aversion to anything that even resembled "settling down" as she'd always known it, this whole fling idea sounded *damn* good.

The trip to Chicago was a short one, so she had to decide quickly. Really, though, she suspected the decision was already made. And as she put her foot on the bottom step and began to climb up, Amanda suddenly had the feeling she was about to embark on the ride of her life.

2

PITTSBURGH TO CHICAGO was a short, easy trip even on a bad day. Fortunately, aside from the fact that he was taking his first flight in a vehicle that didn't look much bigger than his SUV, today was shaping up to be a very good one. And he wasn't just thinking about the weather, which was cool, crisp and clear.

As they took off, Reese went over the situation again in his mind. One hour in the air—that was good. For a mere sixty minutes, he could trick his brain into believing he wasn't *really* sitting inside an oversize tin can, hurtling across a couple of states.

After that, he faced a short taxi ride to the newest location of a brew-pub chain owned by a wealthy Chicago family, the Braddocks. They had recently agreed to offer Campbell's Lager as a house beer in a couple of their bars. It was a foot in the door, and Reese hoped to grow the account and get them to expand their order to include every one of their establishments. So he couldn't refuse when he got a call from old Mr. Braddock himself this morning, asking him to come to put in an appearance at tonight's opening.

He wouldn't have to stay long—just had to shake a

few hands and say a few thank-yous. He should be in and out in under an hour.

And after that…what?

He had intended to hop a commercial flight back to Pittsburgh tonight. The trip had been too impromptu to fly that way this afternoon, but there was one regional jet leaving at 10:00 p.m. that he could undoubtedly find a seat on. If he wanted to.

But ever since he had walked across the tarmac toward the small private plane and seen the woman standing at the base of the steps, he hadn't wanted to. Because one look at her and he'd been interested. One word and he'd been intrigued. And one brief conversation and he'd been utterly hooked.

It wasn't just that she was beautiful. He knew better than to think beauty was ever more than a surface pleasantry. Besides, he was no chauvinist. He had four sisters, three of them unmarried and living at home, the fourth a divorced single mom. Since his brother was only in his early teens, Reese bore the full brunt of female judgment against his sex. The only other adult male in close proximity was Ralph, his black lab, who had lost his claim to maleness at the hands of a ruthless vet when he was just six months old. A female vet.

So, yeah, Reese knew better than to ever judge a woman solely on appearance.

Amanda Bauer's amazing body, her thick reddish-brown hair that hung past her shoulders and her damn-near-perfect face might have stilled his heart for a moment or two. But her smile, her husky voice, the shininess of her green eyes and the snappy humor had brought about the full stop.

So what are you going to do about it?

He needed to decide. And he now had only about forty-five minutes in which to do it.

In any other situation—if they'd met at a business meeting or a local bar—he might not have considered it. He'd been living in a fishbowl for the past two years, with his every move analyzed and dissected by his family. Bringing a woman into the picture was just inviting the kind of microscopic commentary he did not want.

But this was totally different. His pilot was someone he'd never seen before and, after today, probably would never see again. The thought made him suddenly wonder about the ways in which they could spend that day.

Fortunately, thinking about all those things had distracted him from the whole terrifying takeoff business. They'd chatted while she'd prepared for flight, but since the minute the tires had started rolling down the runway, Reese's throat had been too tight to push any words out.

He forced himself to swallow. "So, a full-time pilot, huh?" he asked, knowing the question was an inane one. But it was better than the silence that had fallen between them while she'd been occupied getting them up into the air.

It also beat looking out the window at either the ground, which was getting farther away by the minute, or the wing of the plane, which looked far too small to be the only thing keeping him from a twenty-thousand-foot crash back to mother earth.

He looked away.

"Yep."

"Must be pretty interesting."

"It beats being a kindergarten teacher, which was what my folks wanted me to do."

He barked a laugh. Her. A kindergarten teacher. Right. In his mental list of other careers this woman could have, being a sedate, demure teacher wasn't even in the top gajillion.

Actress. Seductive spy. Rock star. Designer. Sex goddess. Yeah, those he could see. But definitely not teacher.

She glanced back, one brow up, though her tiny smile told him she wasn't truly offended. Reese sat in the first passenger seat on the opposite side of the cabin and their stares locked for just a moment before she faced forward again. "What? You think I couldn't be a teacher?"

"Uh-uh." He quickly held up a defensive hand. "Not that I don't think you're smart enough. You just don't seem the type who'd like working with children."

She did, however, seem the type to be fabulous at the physical act that led to children. Not that he was going to say that to a woman he'd known for less than an hour.

That'd take two, minimum.

"I'm good with kids, I'll have you know," she insisted. "My friends' and cousins' kids love me."

He didn't doubt it. "Because you bring them cool stuff from your travels and you fly an airplane?"

She shrugged, not denying it. Nor did she turn around, keeping her eyes on the sky ahead of her. Which was good. He much preferred his pilot to be on the lookout for any random high-flying helicopters or low-flying space shuttles.

"I'm not knocking it," he said. "I'm the king of doling out loud toys to my sister's kids. I know the gifts will drive her crazy long after I'm gone."

She laughed, low and long, as if reminiscing at some personal memory. Amanda Bauer's warm chuckle seemed to ride across the air inside the cabin and brush against him like a soft breeze on a summer day. He could almost feel it.

Reese shifted in his seat, trying to keep focused on small talk and chitchat. Not on how much he wanted to feel her laughter against his lips so he could inhale the very air she breathed.

"Believe it or not, I think I'd have been a hell of a good teacher."

"Uh-huh. I can hear five-year-old Brittany coming home to tell Mommy she had a hell of a good time learning her ABCs that day."

She still didn't turn around. She didn't have to. Her reaction was made plain by the casual lift of her right hand and the quick flash of her middle finger.

"Hey, both hands on the steering wheel, lady," he said, his shoulders shaking in amusement. His sexy, private pilot had just flipped him off. Damn, he liked this woman. He took no offense. In fact, he was more grateful than anything else that she had already grown so comfortable with him.

It was strange, since they'd just met, but he felt the same way. Oh, not with the fact that he was in a tiny plane far above the ground…but with her. Like he could say just about anything and it would roll off her back. She had such an easygoing way about her. It went well with the adventurous spirit that put her in the cockpit of a plane wearing go-go boots and booty shorts.

Personally, he had the feeling they were going to get along tremendously. He felt more relaxed with her than he had with anyone—including just himself—in months.

Except for the whole being-in-a-small-plane thing. Which he was trying to forget.

"Okay, I apologize," he said. "I'm sure you would have been great. But I think any mother with a brain cell in her head would insist her kid be moved out of your class before the father attended his first parent-teacher conference."

She didn't respond. But the middle finger didn't come up, either.

"Now, back to the subject. Your job. I guess you like to fly, huh?"

Before she could answer, the plane rose suddenly, then dropped hard, though not far, just like a kite being lifted and gently tossed by an unexpected gust. "Jesus…"

"Don't worry, it was just an air pocket. It's completely normal. In a jet this size, we just feel the turbulence a bit more than you're used to."

Why one little pocket of air was any different than the rest of the big, vast atmosphere, he had no idea. He just knew he didn't like it. "Okay, uh, stay away from those pockets, would you please?"

"Sure," she said with a snort and, though he couldn't see it, probably an eye roll. "I'll just watch for the yellow hazard signs and steer around them."

"Your empathy would have been a real help in a job teaching young children."

Instead of being insulted, she snickered, a cute, self-deprecating sound. "Sorry." Then, though she didn't turn completely around, her eyes shifted slightly. Enough to catch a glimpse at his probably tense face. "I like flying better than you, I take it?"

"It's not my favorite thing to do."

"And I bet it's even worse when you're not tucked

inside the belly of a huge 747, trying not to catch the mood of all the other nervous flyers who are envisioning the worst?"

"Exactly."

She nodded once, then offered, "Doesn't it help to think something smaller would be easier to keep aloft than some big, monstrous commercial airliner? Just like a feather on the breeze?"

"No," he admitted. "Actually, all I keep thinking about is the whole man/wings thing."

"Relax. I haven't crashed in, oh, a good month at least."

Not appreciating the joke, he stared, his eyes narrowed. "My luck, I get the comedian in hot pants for the pilot."

"Sorry. Just figured if you laugh a little, you might relax."

"Say something that's actually funny and I might." Though, he doubted it. A tranquilizer or a shot of gin might help him calm down. Or this woman's hands. Then again, if this woman's hands ever did land on him, *calm* almost certainly would not describe his mood.

"Why don't you try closing your eyes and just pretending you're somewhere else?"

"Pretend?"

"You know. Fantasize." Her voice melodic, as if she were a hypnotist, she provided a fantasy. "You're in a safe, solid car driving up a mountain pass toward a beautiful old hotel."

"Okay, this isn't helping. I'm thinking Jack Nicholson heading toward that hotel in *The Shining*."

She huffed out a breath. "It's an exclusive ski lodge,

glamorous, not haunted. Around you is nothing but pristine, white snow, blue sky, clear air."

"Guys with axes…"

"Don't make me come back there!"

"Okay, okay," he said with a grimace.

Reese closed his eyes and tried to see it. He really did. But he could conjure up no mountain pass. No car. No ski lodge.

A curvy snow-bunny wearing a fluffy hat, skimpy shorts and skis…that was about as close as he could get.

He sighed. Not necessarily because it was a bad thing, but because the vision was so damn hot, it had him a little dizzy.

"Don't use your imagination much, I guess. I should have known."

His eyes flew open. "I have an imagination."

"Uh-huh. Let me guess, most of the time what you imagine is getting through the next sales meeting or closing some big business deal."

Reese shifted a little, not answering. Up until he'd walked up to her on the tarmac, that had been pretty accurate. Since then, though, he'd been imagining a few other things. But to tell her she was wrong meant to spill those thoughts, which he wasn't about to do—again, at least not after a one-hour acquaintance.

Though, two was looking better all the time.

The plane bounced again, quickly, up and down. Reese's stomach bounced with it—at least, on the way up. It didn't go all the way down and settle back into place.

He felt the blood drain from his cheeks. "I think we just ran over a moose. Or a lost skier."

"There's a small fridge between the seats. You look like you could use a drink." She chuckled. "Or a Valium."

"Wow. That is first-class service."

"Kidding."

"Yeah. I figured that," he said, ignoring the offer. He didn't need a drink. He just needed a distraction.

Fortunately, one of the sexiest ones he had ever seen was sitting just a few feet away. As long as he didn't humiliate himself by losing his lunch on the floor of her pristine jet, he fully intended to enjoy spending this flight in her company.

And maybe more than that.

After all, why shouldn't he? He already liked her sense of humor, the competent way she handled the controls, the low laughter. There was a lot to like about this woman beyond her killer legs. Not to mention the rest of the physical package. She was quick and witty, sharp, smart. Lots to like. Lots to want.

And he could like her, want her…maybe even have her, without any of the complications that would arise if he were within fifty miles of home. There, he never felt free to do something for no other reason than the fact that he wanted to. The idea of heaving aside all that responsibility for a little while, of grabbing on to a good thing and enjoying the hell out of it just because he *could,* was incredibly appealing.

"Is this your first time chartering?" she asked.

The plane jiggled the tiniest bit and he instinctively clutched the armrests. "That obvious, huh?"

"You have that first-timers glow."

Huh. Did vampires glow? Because he figured his face was probably as white as one.

"Must be a pretty important trip."

He shook his head. "You'd think so, right? But I'm actually headed to a Halloween party."

She glanced over her shoulder in surprise. Reese waved toward the front, "Keep your eyes on the road, please."

"Don't worry. I'm not about to drive into the back of a slow-moving semi doing fifty during rush hour."

He'd just be happy if she didn't drive into the back of a slow-flying goose. A big Canadian one.

Oh, God, one of those had brought down a huge airliner, hadn't it?

Stop thinking about it.

Right. He had much better things to think about. The way his family business was booming under his management, even in this bad economy. The success of their first nationwide marketing campaign. The house he'd just finished remodeling and considered his private fortress in the middle of his crazy world. The sexy pilot in hot pants whom he now kept picturing on skis, and whose downhill slopes he would very much like to explore. Much better things.

"So, Halloween party, huh?" she said. "If this is you dressing up, what do you regularly look like? I mean, in your real life, are you a biker-dude who usually wears black leather and chains? Only for the occasion, you're dressing up as a boring businessman?"

Reese leaned forward, dropping his elbows onto his knees, and stared at the back of her silky-haired head. "Ahem. Boring?"

"It was a joke. I was just trying to distract you."

Maybe. Or maybe she really did think he looked boring.

He should have felt a little insulted. Reese had been fending off most of the single women in his small hometown since his high school days. *Most* of them. He definitely hadn't fended off all, at least not before two years ago when his life had gotten so out of whack. And he had enjoyed his share of discreet flings through the years. Could've had enough to qualify as a half-dozen guys' shares if he'd felt like it. His sisters were forever cackling over some of the ways in which the hungry local females tried to get his attention.

True, the females in question were no longer the twentysomething party girls who'd gone through his revolving bedroom door a few years ago. They were now career women who saw the steady businessman with a nice income and a reputation as being a great guy who stepped up for his family. But there were still quite a few of them and they definitely wouldn't say no if he *ever* started asking again.

He wasn't the hottest dude in the known universe, and he suspected the money that flowed from his family's successful brewery was partially responsible for the attention. But nobody had ever called him boring before, that was for sure.

Damn, that was harsh.

And damn, she was right. To hell with all the mental pumping about how great business was, and how many women had made plays for him. His personal life was *exactly* what this beautiful woman imagined it to be.

Boring.

Boiled in mediocrity and steeped in sameness, he'd allowed himself to disappear into a daily life that wasn't ever what he'd imagined for himself. Ennui had grabbed him by the lapels of his stuffy suit and forced him to remain in his small box of family, business, responsibility. He hadn't even tried to step outside that box in a long time.

Maybe it was time. Maybe he should heed his great-aunt Jean's advice: live, go a little wild, have an adventure.

It had sounded crazy, impossible a few weeks ago when she'd burst into his office. Now? Not so much. Especially because he'd suddenly found someone he wanted to go a little wild with.

There was, of course, one obstacle.

"Are you single?" he asked, direct and to the point.

Her shoulders stiffened the tiniest bit and she hesitated. Then, with a small, shaky exhalation he could hear from back here—as if she'd made some decision—she nodded once.

"Yes. Completely unattached. You?"

"The same."

He didn't give it any more thought. She might have thrown the word *boring* at him, but he had seen the look of interest in her eyes before they'd gotten aboard the plane. The tiny hitch in her breath just now, and the sudden tension that had her curvy body sitting so stiffly in her seat told him her thoughts had gone in the same direction as his.

Have an adventure.

Sounded like a good idea to him.

"So how do you like Halloween parties?"

AMANDA HAD TO ADMIT IT...Reese Campbell made one hot-as-blazes 1970s-era airline pilot. Eyeing him from the other side of the backseat of the taxicab, she wondered what strange whim of fortune had sent such a sexy, charming, single man across her path right when she needed one most.

And she definitely needed one. It had been a long time since she'd felt so sure of herself as a woman, so in tune to the sensations coursing through her body. All the late-night blue movies that had played in her mind lately, replacing any semblance of a real love life, had been mere placeholders, no substitute for the great sex she wasn't having.

Those mental movies were going to have a new leading man in them after tonight. Because she had the feeling that before the night was over, she was going to be saying, "Welcome aboard," and "Fly me," and meaning *exactly* what those old ad execs had wanted passengers to think the sexy stewardesses meant.

She wanted Reese. He wanted her. It was a wild, reckless Halloween night and they were both single and interested.

So why not?

Okay, so she'd never done the one-night-stand-with-an-utter-stranger thing. But her best friend, Jazz, had. She hadn't ended up with a scarlet *A* branded on her chest or any nasty diseases, nor had she needed therapy to get rid of some nonexistent guilt.

Considering she sometimes thought Jazz was the only woman her age in the world who was the least bit like her, or who completely understood her, she didn't figure the example was a bad one to follow.

Besides, Amanda had indulged in short-term affairs before. In fact, considering how badly her last few relationships had ended, a one-night stand sounded just about perfect.

She liked sex. She liked it a lot. This time, she'd just

be having it without the two requisite dates—drinks, then dinner—first. Or the worrying about a phone call the next day. Reese would go back to his life in Pittsburgh, she'd stay here, and they'd both smile whenever they thought of the night they'd gotten a little down-and-dirty with a stranger in Chicago.

Best of all…there'd be no crazy fake suicide attempts. No drunk-dialing complaints that she was a feckless bitch who enjoyed breaking guys' hearts. And Reese wouldn't become the newest member of the Facebook group "Dumped by Amanda Bauer," which had actually been set up by a guy she'd dated during her junior year of college.

God, men could be such fricking babies.

Back to the subject: one-night stand.

Okay. Sounded good. She just had to feel her way around to make sure Reese was on board with it. Judging by the way he'd been devouring her with his eyes since the minute they'd met, she had a feeling that was a big, fat yeah.

"How in God's name did they breathe in these things?" he muttered as he tugged at the too-tight collar of his shirt. "I can't believe there weren't crashes due to lack of oxygen in the pilots' brains."

"It's only a suit, for heaven's sake," she said, rolling her eyes at the typical male grumbling. "It just happens to be too small for you."

They'd found the antique uniform Reese was using as a costume at the airport after landing in Chicago. It hadn't been difficult. Lots of the companies at O'Hare had been around for decades, and Amanda had friends at just about all of them. A few inquiries had put her in the office of a guy who'd worked as a baggage handler since the days when there'd been a Pan in front of American. He'd known where lots of interesting old stuff was kept and had put an only-slightly-musty uniform, complete with jaunty pilot's cap, in her hands within an hour of landing.

It was too tight across Reese Campbell's broad shoulders, but loose around the lean hips and tight buns. Whoever Captain Reliable from the 1970s had been, he definitely hadn't had Reese's mouthwatering build.

"You're going to rip it," she said as he continued to tug. "The thing is flimsy enough."

Brushing his hands away, Amanda reached up to his strong throat, her fingers brushing against the warm, supple skin. A low, deep breath eased in through her nearly closed lips and she suddenly felt a little lightheaded. There was such unexpected strength in him, tone and musculature more suited to an athlete than to the boring businessman she'd accused him of being.

Not that she'd meant it. Not at all. The clothes he'd been wearing might have been conservative, but the look in those eyes, the sexy twist to his lips, the suggestive tone of his conversation...none of those things had indicated anything but exciting, intriguing male.

A thin sheen of sweat moistened the throat where the shirt had cut into the cords of muscle. She had to suck her bottom lip into her mouth just to make sure she didn't do something crazy like lean closer and taste that moisture, sample that skin. She ignored the sudden mental command to just *do* it, focusing instead on unfastening the top button and loosening his tie.

Reese said nothing, just stared at her, his expression hard to read in the low lighting of the cab.

When she was finished, she dropped her hands to her

lap, twisting her fingers together on top of her long winter coat. It didn't quite match the costume, but despite the mild autumn they'd been having, it had become freaking cold out when the sun went down. She honestly didn't know how the hippest 1970s chicks had stood it.

"So, this client of yours, he's not going to mind you showing up with a…" She considered her words, decided against saying *date* and concluded, "…guest?"

"It's a pub," Reese replied, his sensual lips curving up a little at the corners. "I think they can handle one extra."

"That's some job you've got, *having* to go to pubs for Halloween parties," she said, trying to think about something other than his mouth. How much she wanted that mouth. And *where* she wanted that mouth.

"I don't think it quite stacks up to yours—having to jet off to the Caribbean to ferry the rich around to their sinfully expensive vacations."

"I usually ferry obnoxious, spoiled executives to their sinfully expensive corporate retreats."

He tsked. "I'm sure they consider it bailout money well spent." He hesitated for a split second, then added, "So I guess I should be glad you called me boring rather than obnoxious and spoiled?"

"Not obnoxious," she immediately replied.

A brow went up. "Spoiled?"

Amanda tapped her fingertip on her chin, pretending to think about it. She didn't suspect this man was spoiled in the way some of her clients were. He didn't come off as rich, used to everyone bowing down before him at the first request. And he definitely wasn't the kind of guy who expected a woman to spread her legs at the first mention of something sparkly.

Yeah, she'd met a bunch of those guys. Amanda had always been left wondering what kind of woman would trade a night beneath a sweating, out-of-shape, pasty old man for a pair of diamond earrings.

Reese wasn't like those men, not physically, not mentally. She had the feeling he was successful but he was not financially spoiled.

Spoiled in other ways? Maybe. Something about his self-confidence, his half smile when he'd asked if she was single, told her he was used to getting what he wanted when it came to women. The way he sat just a few inches away—casual and comfortable when she, herself, was tingling with excitement at his nearness—said he was sure of what he wanted to happen and his ability to make it happen.

Sexually confident, yeah. *But spoiled?* No. The guy who'd looked like he was going to lose his lunch during the flight had been adorably sexy and vulnerable. Not one creepy, jerky, I'm-good-and-I-know-it thing about him.

"Not spoiled," she admitted.

"I should hope not. As the oldest of six kids, I learned at a very young age not to count on anything I owned remaining unbroken, unborrowed or unlost."

"Six kids!" The very idea horrified her. One sibling— one perfect, good, just-like-their-parents sibling who did exactly what was expected of her and never stepped off the approved path—was quite enough for Amanda, thank you very much.

"My God. Six. I can't even imagine it," she muttered.

"Oh yeah." A small chuckle emerged from his mouth as he added, "It was never *boring*."

Amanda nibbled her bottom lip before replying, a bit sheepishly, "Sorry I said that earlier. I was just trying to get you to relax."

Reese might dress the part of executive, but no man with those looks, that mouth and that gleam of interest in his eyes could possibly be called boring.

"So how's that strategy work for you?"

Confused, she asked, "What strategy?"

"Throwing insults at guys to relax them. Working out okay?"

Hearing the laughter in his tone—knowing he was laughing at himself, too—she had to admit, she liked Reese Campbell.

Wanted him. Liked him. Two points checked off her mental I'm-no-slut-and-don't-have-one-night-stands list.

Tonight was looking better by the minute.

"It worked on me, by the way." He leaned back farther in the seat, turning a little to stare at her. The dim reflections from streetlights they passed striped his handsome features in light and shadow. His breaths created tiny vapors in the chilly air that couldn't be banished by the car's weakly blowing heater. His voice was low, thick as he promised, "Because I'm looking forward to proving you wrong, Amanda."

Her heart skipped a beat. Just one. Something about the way her name rode softly, smoothly, on his exhalation, thrilled her. But she managed to keep her own breaths even. "Oh?"

He nodded. "There's nothing boring about what's going to happen between us."

A shiver of excitement coursed through her. It started with her lips, which quivered and parted, then moved down her entire body, which suddenly felt so much more…alert, somehow. The cold was more biting, the coat scratchy against her bare thighs. Her breasts tingled under the slick, polyester fabric of her blouse, the sensation sensual against her tight nipples.

Excitement had awakened every inch of her. It had been there, sparking right beneath the surface, for hours, since she'd first spied him on that tarmac back in Pittsburgh. Now the spark had caught and spread into a wildfire of interest and arousal, even though he hadn't touched her.

He knew. He had to know. The very air seemed thick with her sudden certainty of just how much she wanted the man. That certainty must have communicated itself to him with her shallow, audible breaths, the almost imperceptible way she leaned closer to him, irresistibly drawn to his heat. His size. His scent.

The big, strong hand sliding into her hair and cupping her head came as no surprise. She smiled in anticipation as he turned her face, tilted her chin up, then bent toward her. Their breaths mingled in the cold evening air and an almost tangible sizzle of excitement preceded the initial meeting of their lips.

A heartbeat later, the cold air disappeared. Nothing separated them at all.

Their first kiss was no tentative brush of lip on lip, nor was there any hesitation, or even a gasp at the thrill of it. It was instead strong and wet. Sensuous. Confident and hungry, Reese parted his lips and slid his tongue against hers, tasting deeply, thoroughly, with enjoyment but not desperation.

Enjoyment could easily lead to desperation, she had no doubt. But despite the fact that they were in the backseat of a random cab, and had a one-man audience, courtesy of the rearview mirror, Amanda didn't care.

She wanted this. Craved it. So she didn't resist or even hesitate. Instead, she reacted with pure instinct, wrapping her arms around his neck. Tilting her head to the side, she silently invited him deeper. She moaned at the delights provided by his soft tongue, tasting him and exploring the inside of his mouth.

He was warm and solid, the spicy, masculine smell of him filling her head even as his heat against her body chased away any last remnants of chill.

Finally, he ended the kiss, slowly pulling away far enough to stare down into her eyes. She saw want there. And something else—excitement. Pleasure.

His lips quirked. And she saw even more: self-confidence. He confirmed it with a broad, satisfied smile.

"This is going to be so much fun."

"The party?"

He shook his head. "You and me."

3

ALMOST FROM THE MOMENT they'd met, Reese had known he was heading in one direction: toward Amanda Bauer's bed.

They were going to have sex. Soon.

Reese knew it. Amanda knew it. The two of them were savoring that knowledge, building the anticipation as the evening wore on.

He'd done his bit for the business. Then, when old Mr. Braddock and his family had left for the night, he'd taken off his official Campbell's Lager title and gone back to being Reese, the man who'd picked up his sexy personal pilot.

Every look asked and answered the same question. Every smile was a seduction, each casual word a hidden code and every brief brush of hand on hand had become the most sensual foreplay. The way they intentionally tried *not* to touch more intimately increased the incredible tension, each non-caress promised unimaginable pleasure when they finally did come together.

Reese couldn't remember a time in his life when he'd been more excited by a woman. He just knew, as he stared at her across the crowded bar, that he'd never desired one more.

They hadn't kissed again since that brief encounter in the cab. They hadn't needed to. The want they were both feeling had been building by the minute.

When they'd danced, and his hand cupped her hip, or her thigh slid against his, the anticipation of how this night was going to end had nearly sent him out of his mind.

It had also sent him in search of something to try to calm down his body's heated reactions.

"So, are you supposed to be, like, the president or something?"

Reese didn't bother glancing over at the vapid little redhead dressed as a sex kitten—one of at least a dozen in the packed-to-bursting bar. She'd been trying to engage him in conversation for a full minute, but he was busy focusing on the dance floor. And frowning.

Because there, in the middle of a writhing crowd full of zombies and witches, mad scientists and vampy angels, was his sexy stewardess…dancing with another guy. He'd made his move when Reese had gone in search of a cold shower, but had had to make do with a cold glass of water.

"Or, like, a James Bond spy?"

Right. 'Cause James Bond always wore stupid navy blue uniforms and captain's wings on his lapel.

"You're way too hot to be an accountant or something."

"Pilot," he mumbled, barely paying attention. All his attention was focused on Amanda.

She looked better than any woman in the place as she shook her stuff with a man Reese recognized as one of

Braddock's low-level employees. Steve something or other.

Reese had never had a problem with him—at least not until he'd realized Steve was seriously moving in on his date.

Steve hadn't been able to keep his covetous eyes off Amanda since the minute they'd arrived. Reese had figured the hands-off-she's-here-with-someone-else code would prevent the other man from actually doing anything about it. But when Steve's hand accidentally brushed Amanda's luscious ass for a second time, Reese realized he was either too drunk, or too hot for her, to even remember the code.

He tensed, ready to stride out there and do something that could cost his company a major customer, depending on how much Mr. Braddock liked Steve, even as he wondered what this crazy, unfamiliar jealousy was all about. But before he could do anything, the redheaded feline jiggled around in front of him, purring, "Dance with me?"

She didn't wait for an answer, just grabbed his arm and tugged him forward. He wasn't the first man she'd been gyrating up against tonight. An hour ago, she'd been wrapped around some guy dressed as a caveman, complete with fur loincloth. Captain Caveman was now groping a woman in a Little Red Riding Hood costume cut so low it barely covered her nipples.

Was there a law somewhere that said Halloween costumes for twenty-something-year-old women had to be slutty? God, he hated parties like this. How could he possibly have forgotten?

The only good thing about tonight's was the moment he and Amanda had hit the dance floor themselves. After he'd officially gone "off duty" they'd had a couple of drinks. Drifting into the crowd, they'd danced not to the loud music, but to the intimate, primal beat that had been thrumming between them for hours.

He should never have left her alone. He should have just lived with the hard-on, trusting that the crowd on the dance floor would ensure nobody else knew he was dying to rip his date's hot pants off and screw her into incoherence.

"C'mon, it's a party, in case ya haven't noticed!"

The redhead was the one who wasn't too observant. She obviously didn't notice that every ounce of his attention was focused on another woman. Or else she just didn't care. He figured that was it because she had dragged him to within a few feet of Amanda and Steve, then proceeded to pole dance against his thigh, rubbing so hard he could feel the heat of her crotch through both sets of their clothes.

Nasty.

Grabbing her shoulders to push her off, he grimaced when she reached up and clasped onto his hand. Holding tight, she then turned her head and tried to suck his thumb into her mouth.

Repeat: You hate Halloween parties. And he was so far over the bar scene, he honestly couldn't remember why he'd once enjoyed it.

Before he could disentangle himself, he glanced over and met Amanda's stare. Her eyes narrowed and hardened. Her pretty lips compressed as she saw the strange young woman practically riding him, the pouty suction-cup mouth trying to simulate a sex act on his thumb.

He knew how it must look—as if he was pulling the bimbo closer rather than pushing her away. Amanda obviously saw it that way, because she rolled her eyes and grimaced, her jaw rock-hard and her slim form straight and tense. Considering she had been fending off the groping hands of one of Reese's customers, she had every right to be angry as hell.

Reese was on the verge of just sacrificing his thumb to death-by-the-jaws-of-drunk-ho and pushing over to Amanda's side. He needed to explain, and to get her the hell out of there. But she suddenly changed the game. With a look that verged between anger and challenge, she wrapped her arms around Steve's neck. She slid closer to him, swaying slowly to the pounding music that had everyone else gyrating and bouncing. Steve all but stumbled as her beautiful mouth came close to his neck. Over the other man's shoulder, her stare sought out Reese's and she lifted one brow in a deliberate taunt.

Damn. She was tormenting him. His sexy pilot had claws much sharper than this intoxicated little cat who was still trying to use his thigh as a scratching post and, now, his neck as a lump of catnip.

He should have been annoyed—he'd never liked women who played games. But somehow, as his heart started thudding hard against his rib cage and all his blood again rushed to his cock, he realized he was incredibly excited by Amanda Bauer instead.

Their stares locked, intense and hot. She licked her lips, and Steve tugged her closer, as if he'd almost felt that sweet, wet tongue. But her attention wasn't on Steve, it was entirely on Reese. Her eyes sparkled, as if she knew he was torn between wanting to laugh at her for trying to make him jealous or pick her up, throw her over his shoulder and out-caveman the guy in the loincloth.

Reese lifted a questioning brow, silently asking her

how far she was going to take this. In response, she leaned toward Steve's ear and whispered something. The other man froze, dropping his arms and watching as Amanda turned away from him. She eased through the crowd, winding a path across the dance floor, heading toward a back hallway that led to the restrooms. A number of men turned to watch her go, and she earned more than a few glares from their dates. Just before she slipped down the short hallway, she cast one more glance over her shoulder. Her half smile taunted Reese, daring him to follow.

Reese spun the horny little cat around and pushed her toward the still-frozen Steve, who appeared almost shell-shocked. When he met Reese's eyes, he flushed, then mumbled, "Sorry, man."

Whatever Amanda had said, it had worked. He should have known she needed no help in taking care of herself. Still, he couldn't help smiling tightly and saying, "I think my date and I will be leaving now. Before you do something that requires me to break your jaw."

Not waiting for a reply, Reese moved in the same direction Amanda had gone. Easier said than done, as the dance floor swelled when the deejay put on a campy version of the "Monster Mash." He couldn't find an inch of clear space and had to push his way through couple after couple.

Finally, though, he reached the short hallway. A woman had just disappeared into the ladies' room, and a guy in a toga passed him as he left the men's. Stepping into a corner to wait, he started when he felt a hand on his shoulder.

"I knew you'd follow me," a throaty voice whispered.

Amanda.

She'd appeared from the shadows of a storage room, ignoring the Private: Employees Only sign. Standing in the doorway, she watched him with heat in her green eyes and a pant of audible hunger flowing across her moist lips.

"I knew you wanted me to."

He didn't resist when she tugged him inside the small room, dark, damp, smelling of yeasty beer and booze.

"Your girlfriend isn't going to come after us, is she?" Amanda whispered as she pushed the door shut behind him, trapping them inside.

He made sure everyone else was kept out by twisting the lock on the knob. "My girlfriend?"

She reached up and ran the tip of one index finger over his bottom lip, hissing lightly when he nipped at it. "Uh-huh. She looks very *catty*." Leaning up on tiptoe, she pressed her wet lips to his throat, swiping her small tongue against the hollow. "I don't usually go after other girls' guys but the way you've been looking at me all night has me feeling a little reckless."

He got into the spirit of her game. "She's not the one I want." Reese stared down at her, able to see her beautiful face more clearly as his eyes adjusted to the glimmer of moonlight spilling in from a small window. He leaned into her, knowing by her groan that she felt his raging erection pressing into the juncture of her thighs. "She's not the one who's had me hard and desperate for the past six hours." Being honest now, he added, "You're a stranger and yet I'm dying for you."

She lifted one slim leg, tilting toward him so his cock nested against the warm seam of her silky hot pants. He swallowed hard, desperately wanting to yank down his zipper, tear her shorts off and thrust into her hard, fast and deep. But a bigger part of him wanted it slow and hot, erotic as hell, with every sensation building upon the last, until the tension of anticipation had them both ready to explode.

"Sex with a stranger is a very enticing fantasy, isn't it?" she asked. "How lucky that we saw each other across the bar and both knew exactly what we had to have."

Wicked. Erotic. So damned sexy.

"Aren't you afraid your boyfriend is going to come looking for you?" He was half-curious about what she'd said to the other man before abandoning him. But not curious enough to ask, or do anything that might distract them from what was happening right here, right now.

"I don't care," she mumbled, her fingers tugging at his tie, slipping the top button of his shirt open. "He can't satisfy me."

Her fingertips brushed his bare chest and he hissed at the sensation of skin on skin. "No. He can't. But believe me, I'm going to."

Hearing the sexy confidence in Reese Campbell's voice, Amanda melted a little. Okay, a lot. Coming from another guy—like the drunk ass she'd just ditched on the dance floor—the pronouncement might have come off as arrogant. But to her ears, Reese's certainty about the pleasure he intended to give her was utterly intoxicating. There was no conceit in it; he simply knew, as she did, that their chemistry was enough to take them both to places neither of them had ever gone before.

"One thing we have to make clear up front," she said, staring up at him, dropping the game for a moment.

"Yes?"

"This is just a one-night stand."

Instead of taking offense, he laughed softly. "Why don't you wait until after you've actually tasted something off the menu before deciding whether or not you want dessert?"

"I suspect you're going to fill me up very nicely the first time," she said, trying to sound seductive but knowing that had come out almost prim.

His continued laughter confirmed it.

She nibbled her bottom lip, her heart beating in excitement at all the ways she wanted to taste him. But the demands of her job, her travel, her commitment to the company and her allergy to anything resembling a relationship made her persist.

"I'm not looking for anything serious or long-term. No entanglements."

Sounding almost relieved, he replied, "Then we're on the same page. My life is so full of people right now, the Health Department is gonna cite me for over-crowding."

She hammered the point home. "So we're clear. One night, then it's done. We'll just enjoy ourselves because it's a holiday and we're both unattached and we want each other. We play all night and then walk away in the morning?"

"Sure," he said with a half grin that promised he didn't really mean it. But she had the feeling it was as close to a promise as he intended to give her.

"Okay. Good…perfect."

He stared at her in the darkness, running the tip of his index finger across her cheek. "Yeah. Perfect. That's exactly the word I'd use."

For her? For them? For this moment and this night

and this wonderful, unexpected interlude? All of the above?

Who gave a damn?

"I want you, stranger," she said, feeling bold, crazy, wild with need and want. "I want you *now*."

He groaned, sinking his hands into her hair, tugging her face to his to capture her mouth in a deep, hard kiss. Without breaking away, he maneuvered her around so her back was to the door, and he crowded her there. Every inch of her body was enveloped by his, every curve, angle and point, and she whimpered and writhed at the feeling of being so utterly in his control.

She wasn't used to the sensations, had never been so enslaved by a person, a feeling, a need. She felt powerless, immobilized, able only to enjoy what he was doing to her, give herself over completely to his every sensual whim.

Somehow, she just didn't care. Maybe because she had gone for so long without any kind of physical connection. Or because it was Halloween and she was dressed in a crazy costume. Or that she had never played sexy, sultry games like they were engaging in tonight and had suddenly discovered she liked them. Or simply that she found Reese more attractive and exciting than any man she had ever met. It didn't matter.

This mattered. Just this.

"Please," she whispered, not even sure what she was asking for.

Moving his mouth to her jaw, he pressed hot kisses to her even hotter skin. He tasted her neck, before traveling on to her pulse point and licking lightly. "Have I told you that I really like your costume?"

That mouth moved lower, down to her nape, and he

scraped his teeth across her collarbone, ever so lightly. She shivered. Ever so lightly.

"I do, too," she admitted, meaning it. Arching against him, she groaned at the feel of her own silky blouse against her hard, sensitive nipples. The hot pants had never felt so tight, and the seam did wonderfully wicked things to her highly sensitized clit.

"I think I'll like it even more when it's on the floor." His strong hands moved down, brushing her shoulders, sliding the length of her arms. His fingertips brushed hers in a caress so light and delicate she shivered with the need for more.

He cupped her hips, holding her in place. Pressed against him, she almost cried with the need to see, feel, taste and be filled by the massive erection pressed into her groin.

"Don't you think we should hurry before somebody comes looking for us?" she asked, helpless and desperate for him to go faster. Harder. Now.

"Nobody's going to come looking for us."

She wasn't giving up. "Not even your girlfriend?"

He smiled a little, his white teeth gleaming in the low lighting. "Oh, we have a very open relationship. She told me to come back here and have a fabulous time with you, then tell her all about it."

God, he was so sexy, tempting her with all that was forbidden and hot. He was still playing, but changing the rules of the game to suit his whim. He made it more taboo, more erotic.

"So does that mean you like handling two women at the same time?" she asked, intentionally trying to inflame him. She wanted him to go faster, give her more, *immediately*.

She should have known better. Reese merely continued to kiss her mouth, her jaw, her earlobe. "I'd like to have two yous."

"Why don't you have one me first before deciding whether you want a double portion?"

Though he chuckled, Reese continued to take his time, dragging this out. He was going to torture her with a slow, seductive ignition rather than just making her explode in a hot, sexual inferno the way she wanted him to.

"You evil man," she muttered.

Reese moved his mouth back to her throat, kissing his way down, licking, nibbling. Amanda could only wriggle and moan as sensations washed over her. When his rough cheek brushed the upper curve of one breast, she instinctively arched toward him, wanting a much more intimate connection.

Reese complied, rubbing his cheek against the silky blouse as he moved his mouth to her nipple. He breathed over it, hot and anticipatory, then covered the taut peak and sucked her through the material.

"You wonderful man," she groaned.

Her legs going weak, she sagged against him. His body in front of her and the door at her back seemed to be the only things holding her up.

As much as she wanted him to, he didn't pull her blouse open and suckle her bare breast, seeming content to torment her through her clothes.

"Reese, touch me, please," she whispered.

He *was* touching her, gripping her hips, his fingertips digging lightly into her bottom. But she wanted so much more.

Reese's strong hands traveled up her sides in a slow,

deliberate slide. The palms nestled in the indentation of her waist, cupped tenderly, then rose to her midriff, right beside her breasts.

"Beautiful," he murmured as he tightened his hands, plumping her breasts up so the top curves almost spilled free of the blouse. Then the ancient top button gave way, popping open. He took immediate advantage, lowering his face and nuzzling against her, even as he worked the next button free, and the one below that.

When the silky blouse fell off her shoulders, Reese stepped back so he could look down at her, his appreciative stare turning into one of pure, raging hunger. This time, she didn't have to ask him to touch her, taste her. Instead, he immediately bent down, covering a nipple with his mouth and sucking hard.

She tangled her hands in his hair, holding him there, feeling every deep pull right down to the quivering spot of sensation between her thighs. Tweaking her other breast with his hand, he rolled the tip between his fingertips. A firm pluck brought a shaky cry to her lips. Reese moved his mouth over to kiss and suck away any twinge of pain, though he knew—he had to know—that what she felt was utter pleasure.

Desperate for skin-on-skin contact, she yanked at his shirt, pulling it apart, not giving a damn that a few buttons went flying. He didn't seem to care, either. He simply shrugged out of it, continuing the lovely, erotic attention to her breasts.

Then, once he, too, was bare from the waist up, he moved back to her mouth and kissed her deeply. Their tongues tangled and played as their bare chests sizzled against one another. She didn't know that she'd ever felt anything as delicious as the crisp hairs on his chest scraping across her moist nipples.

Except, perhaps, for his mouth. And his hands. And, she suspected, just about anything else he chose to press against her in the next fifteen minutes.

They didn't end the kiss, not even when they each reached for the other's waistbands. His deft fingers easily unfastened her hot pants, and his costume was so loose on him, she only had to unbutton, not unzip, before she was able to push the trousers down over his lean hips.

He'd had something on under his clothes—boxer briefs that strained to contain an erection that literally made her suck in a shocked, delighted breath.

All that hugeness. All hers. At least for tonight.

Before he let the pants fall away, he reached into the pocket. "I hope you don't think I was taking you for granted, but I bought this from a machine in the men's room."

She saw him tug the condom from his pocket and grinned. "My purse is over there. And if you look inside, you'll see that I stopped at the airport gift shop and bought an entire box. So I think I'm the one who could be accused of taking you for granted."

"Anytime, anywhere, beautiful."

She liked the way he called her that, liked the way he silently repeated it with his eyes as he stared at her. His gaze was covetous as he stepped back enough to look down at her middle, her hips, the juncture of her thighs.

That look was so hungry, she should have been warned about what he was going to do. But she wasn't. It took her completely by surprise when he dropped to his knees on the bare cement floor and pressed his mouth to the hollow just below her pelvic bone. Then his soft, seeking tongue was dipping low, licking the moisture off her damp curls.

Oral sex was, to quote the song, one of her favorite things. But she had never gotten it quite so quickly from a man. Or quite so….

"Oh, God," she groaned when he moved lower, sliding that warm, sweet tongue between the lips of her sex and swirling it around her throbbing clit. "That's fantastic."

She sagged against the door, helpless to do anything else under the onslaught of such intense pleasure. And she didn't make a sound of protest when he encircled one of her bare limbs with a big, strong hand. Without a word, he guided it over his shoulder, tilting her sex even closer to his hungry mouth.

"Reese, you don't have to…"

"Yeah, actually I do," he mumbled, continuing what he was doing.

She looked down at him, seeing her own booted foot resting against his back. Only now it looked incredibly hot and sexy, the ultimate do-me boots from the original era of free love.

She suddenly felt like the girl she'd been portraying. Like she was some sexy stewardess having a crazy closet interlude with a pilot, just because she *wanted* to. No explanations, no questions, no regrets. Live in the moment and love the one you're with.

Sounded pretty damn fine to her.

"Stop thinking. Let go," he ordered, not looking up.

Amanda did what he asked, giving up any effort to pretend she didn't want him to finish what he'd started.

Finish it he did. Within moments, she felt the sparking, zinging waves of heated delight that had been focusing tightly in on her clit turn around and explode outward. They rocketed through her entire body, wave upon wave, delighting her to the tips of each strand of hair.

Amanda cried out, rocking her hips. He stayed with her, continuing to taste her as she rode the orgasm out, milking it and squeezing her muscles tight to wring out every last bit of sensation. And only after it was over did he slide out from under her leg and ease his way up her naked body.

She was panting and nearly desperate by the time his face was level with hers. His eyes gleaming, he licked at his moist lips and whispered, "Definitely want to keep ordering off this menu."

Dying for him now, needing to be filled, she grabbed two handfuls of his hair and pulled his face to hers for a deep, drugging kiss. This time, she was the one who lifted her leg. Wrapping it around his thighs, she tilted her groin against that thick erection still covered by his briefs.

"Off," she ordered, mumbling the command against his mouth.

He moved a few inches away, far enough to strip out of the last of his clothes. Far enough for Amanda to look down and take measure of the delightful present that was headed her way.

Whoa. As she'd suspected, Reese's "present" was far greater than any she'd ever seen before. She nearly panted with the need to have all that male heat slamming into her, filling the hollow core that had practically grown dusty with disuse.

"Damn. I wasn't exaggerating," she whispered.

He didn't even glance up, tearing the condom open with his teeth and rolling it onto his cock as he mumbled, "Hmm?"

"I told that jerk on the dance floor that if he thought he could measure up to you, he obviously needed to get a new ruler because his had to be broken."

He barked a laugh, but that immediately faded when he moved between her thighs. Amanda lifted her leg again, opening for him, arching toward the massive tip and rubbing her body's natural juices over it.

He put a hand on the door behind her head, palm flat, his strong arm just above her shoulders. She turned her head for a moment, wanting to taste his wrist, feel his blood pounding in his veins. She did so, licking the sweat off him, feeling the strength of his pulse against her tongue. His excitement merely fueled her own as she looked back up into his face, losing herself in those blue eyes.

Their stare never broke as he eased into her. He moved slowly, with utter restraint. Amanda's mouth fell open with a tiny gasp at the feel of him as he went deeper, inch by inch. He was solid and thick, stretching her, making a place for himself within her body.

A temporary one, she knew that. But she also knew it was one she would never *ever* forget. This was the one-night lover every woman fantasized about at least once in her life. And for tonight, he was hers.

"Perfect," he said, echoing his earlier claim.

This time, she knew what he was talking about. Knew as he slid home, burying himself to the hilt inside her, that he meant their connection was perfect. Being joined with him felt about as wonderful as anything on this earth possibly could.

"You okay?"

She nodded, unable to speak. Sensations battered her, his smell, the heat of his skin against hers, his warm breaths against her cheek. She even felt his heartbeat, realizing at once that its rhythm was perfectly matched to her own, as if they shared one single organ.

"Perfect," she finally agreed.

As if he'd been waiting for her, to make sure she was really okay with his incredibly deep possession, Reese finally began to move. He dropped his hands to her hips, holding her still as he slowly withdrew, then slid into her again, making her feel so damn good she let out a tiny sob.

The next thrust was a little harder. The one after that harder still. Each wrung a louder groan from her throat.

"More," she ordered, digging her hands into his broad shoulders, still stunned by the strength of the body he'd hidden beneath that conservative suit.

"You got it."

He lifted her, his hands holding her bottom, controlling every thrust, every move, every sensation. Wrapping her legs around his hips, Amanda kissed his cheeks, stroked his hair and held on while he brought her to another intense orgasm.

It rocked her, hard. She threw her head back and cried out, banging into the door but not really caring. Nor did she care when Reese seemed to lose whatever remnants of control had been restraining him. As if her cries of pleasure had stripped away his every thought, he drove into her mindlessly, until finally, with a cry that was twice the volume of her own, he climaxed, too.

He held her there for a long time, still inside her, his breath sounding ragged and his heart pounding crazily against hers. Finally, though, he let her down to stand on her own two shaky legs.

He didn't let her loose entirely, keeping his arms draped around her shoulders. Finally, after a few minutes during which her pulse dropped back from the red zone to orange, he lifted a hand to her face and cupped her chin.

"Amanda?"

"Yeah?"

"Where do you live?"

"I have an apartment not too far from here."

He nodded, then disentangled himself from her with one last, regretful caress. "Let's get dressed. Or, get as dressed as we can given the missing buttons." He stared at her intently, as if he were looking for some clue to her mood. "If you really meant it, if we've only got one night…"

Her heart skipped a beat. She knew what he was asking. Did she *really* want to stick to that original condition?

Oh, God, was she tempted to tell him to forget what she'd said. Having had him once, it seemed almost inconceivable that she wouldn't have him again after tonight.

But a small voice inside her head—the one that kept reminding her of just how badly every one of her previous affairs had ended—wouldn't let her do it. So she said nothing.

He nodded once, then pressed a hard kiss on her lips.

"Got it." He handed her her clothes and began pulling on his, as well. "Let's hurry up, then. If we've only got this one night, I want to spend as much of it as I possibly can in your bed…making love to you."

Her hand shook a little. Because with those words, those sexy, tender words, a sneaking suspicion crossed her mind.

One night was not going to be enough.

4

Veterans Day

From: mandainflight@hotmail.com
To: Rcampbell@campbelllagers.com
Sent: Tuesday, Nov 10, 2009
Subject: One more time?
Reese—
Another holiday...whaddya say? Want to meet
me for a Veterans Day game of captured enemy
soldier vs. ruthless interrogator?
Manda

From: Rcampbell@campbelllagers.com
To: mandainflight@hotmail.com
Sent: Tuesday, Nov 10, 2009
Subject: One more time?
Affirmative. Where. When.
R.
PS: Tell me I get to be the ruthless interrogator.

BEING INTERROGATED had never been so much fun.
  Lying in bed in the Cleveland hotel room, Reese

watched as the sexiest woman he knew emerged from the bathroom. She was wrapped in a white towel, her skin slick and reddened from the steamy hot shower she'd just taken. It was probably also that way because he'd been touching her, tasting her, adoring her all afternoon. And though he'd already spent almost as many waking hours today inside her body as he had out of it, he already wanted her again.

He still couldn't quite believe this had even happened. Not the sex—God, yes, that was bound to happen whenever the two of them were in a room with a flat surface. But them being together again at *all*.

He'd tried calling Amanda a couple of times after they'd said their goodbyes in Chicago the morning after Halloween. She hadn't responded. Nor had she returned his e-mails.

Finally, he'd had to accept the fact that she'd meant it—one night only. He'd have to live for the rest of his life with the knowledge that the most desirable woman he'd ever met, and the best sex he'd ever had, were both in his past.

He'd tried to get his mind back into his real life. So much needed his attention: the business, the family, his own house. Responsibilities seemed to weigh heavier on his back every time he answered the phone or opened his front door.

Then, out of the blue, this morning, her message.

He hadn't hesitated. Inventing an out-of-town meeting, he'd thrown a few things in a bag, dropped his dog off at a buddy's and headed to Cleveland. He'd needed no further details than the name of the hotel and the time she'd be there.

There was nothing that could have prevented him

from making the trip. Absolutely nothing that would have stopped him from accepting her invitation to sin.

And oh, sin they had.

"You know, I might have been lying about where the top-secret orders were hidden. They might not really be inside Jimi Hendrix's guitar at the Rock and Roll Hall of Fame. Maybe you should torture me again to get the truth out of me," he offered.

Reaching for her purse, Amanda grabbed a hairbrush from within it, and turned to face the mirror. She caught his eye in the reflection as she began to brush the wet strands. "Sorry. Not buying it. I don't think anybody could have held out against that last round of—" she licked her lips "—questioning."

God. He began to harden again, just at the thought of it. That last round of *questioning* had been unforgettable.

Well, to be honest, the whole afternoon had been unforgettable.

She'd been playing her role from the minute he'd walked through the door of the hotel room. He was her prisoner and he had to do what she said. He'd gone along, liking the wildness in her. She was aggressive, demanding. So damned sexy.

Amanda had insisted that he strip. Threatening to punish him if he didn't cooperate, she had then instructed him to sit in a chair right beside the head of the bed.

Half curious, more than half turned-on, he'd agreed to her terms. He wanted to see how far she would go, just what she had in mind. So he'd given his word he would not rise from that chair, no matter what she said or did.

He'd been certain he could do it. Absolutely positive.

He'd told himself he wouldn't get up, not even if the room caught fire.

Then it did. Or, at least, she'd made it *feel* that way, filling the place with so much intense heat he'd thought his skin was going to peel off his bones.

It took every bit of his strength to remain still, just an observer. Because with pure wickedness in her eyes, Amanda had slowly slid out of her clothes and gotten comfortable on the bed, directly in front of him. There she'd proceeded to thoroughly pleasure herself.

Seeing her hands move over that amazing body, being an observer, unable to participate, had been *exactly* the torture she'd anticipated. He'd begun to sweat, to pant, to strain and to clench his fists in a quest for control.

Not content to just run her hand across her bare breast or delicately stroke her long fingertips over her gleaming slit, she'd actually pulled out a vibrating sex toy. He'd had to sit there, silent, nearly dying, while she'd used it to bring herself to orgasm three times.

Then, still ordering him to stay still and leave everything in her control, she'd climbed on top of him and slid down onto his shaft, taking him deep inside her body, controlling their every move, every thrust, every stroke. At one point she'd even turned around to ride him like a cowgirl, all while smiling at his reflection in the same damn mirror she was using now.

He was pretty sure he'd come at least a gallon when she finally did let him go over the edge with her. And that had been only the beginning.

"You're incredible."

"Must be Stockholm Syndrome," she quipped. "You're infatuated with your captor, right?"

"Uh-huh." *Infatuated*. Good word. Maybe even on the verge of obsessed.

"Don't worry, it'll pass."

He very much doubted it. "I don't think so."

Her smile faded a little at his intense tone, and her eyes shifted as she busied herself finishing her hair. He suddenly wondered if he'd touched a nerve.

"You might say you like all of me, but I bet there are certain parts you like better than others." She pursed those lips, reminding him of everything else they'd done so far today. Amanda's second round of torment had involved her luscious mouth.

He had loved giving her oral sex their first time. But Reese had never even contemplated how mind-blowing it would be when she wrapped her lips around his cock. Again and again, she'd brought him to the very edge, taking him as close to orgasm as she could get him, then backing off, cooling things down.

He'd held out as long as he could, liking this reckless, wild side of her. Not to mention loving the feel of her lips and tongue sucking him into oblivion. Finally, though, it had gone too far and he knew he couldn't wait much longer. So he'd played his role in the game, giving her the "information" she had been asking for.

But instead of ending it, pulling him down on top of her so he could finish things in the sweet channel between her legs, she'd ended the game with her mouth. She hadn't even given him the chance to do the polite guy thing—or the standard porn movie one—and pull out before reaching the end of the countdown.

Wild. Erotic. Intense.

She was his every fantasy. And about as far from his real life as a woman could possibly be.

He forcibly pushed that thought away. Because, though they'd done almost no talking so far today, he didn't imagine Amanda's feelings about what they were doing—and what they were going to do in the future— had changed. A one-night stand had evolved into a holiday affair. He just didn't know how far out on the calendar she'd want to go. She might be his Thanksgiving feast or his ultimate Christmas present. If fate was kind, perhaps she'd be the one coloring his Easter eggs.

Or they might have tonight and nothing else. Ever.

Not knowing drove him crazy, in both a good way and a bad one. The possibility that this might be all made him desperate to have and take and possess her as much as he could.

It's not all. It can't be all.

"I'm hungry," she said.

Thrusting away his thoughts of tomorrow, he knew he had to focus on tonight. He rolled over to sit up on the edge of the bed. One thing was sure—he needed to eat in order to have the strength to spend the rest of the night the way he wanted. "Me, too. Please tell me I've been cooperative enough to get more than bread and water."

"How's cold gruel sound?"

"Uh-uh. I need protein. Let me take you out to dinner."

Her mouth fell open, but quickly snapped closed again. After a hesitation, she murmured, "I don't know…"

"I've got to keep up my strength. How else can I hope to resist you?"

Her head turned a little and she averted her gaze. "Resist me? That's what you call resisting?"

"Come on, cut me a break. It's kinda hard to say no to a woman when she has your cock in her mouth."

Amazing. They'd done the most intense things to one another, but he'd swear a slight flush rose in her face at his words. And she still wouldn't look at him.

Embarrassment? That seemed crazy, given all they'd shared. Besides, her unease hadn't started with his crass comment, but when he'd suggested that they go out to eat. Or maybe a few minutes before that when he'd admitted to being infatuated with her.

"Let's stay in. We can order room service," she insisted.

She'd play sex games with him all afternoon, but didn't want to go on anything resembling a date?

Interesting.

Reese stood and walked up behind her, dropping his hands to her hips and pressing a kiss on her nape. "Room service for breakfast," he whispered. "Tonight, though, let's get out of here for a little while."

She still looked uncertain. As if, now that the game was over, now that they were played-out and talking about something as simple as food, she didn't know what to say, how to act.

Or who to be.

"We both know that's not what this is about..."

"Look, I'm not proposing, okay?" he said, forcing a noncommittal laugh. "It's dinner. Eating together, not any kind of a declaration. Sharing a meal doesn't elevate this to anything more than the two-night stand you've decided we can have."

Her eyes flared in surprise, as if she hadn't guessed how easy she was to read.

Reese shrugged. "I'm not stupid, okay? I know what

you want, and what you don't. I accepted that when I showed up here today."

She still hesitated.

"No pressure, no hidden meanings, just food," he said, coaxing her as carefully as he would a wild bird with a piece of bread. "You can choose where we go. As long as it's someplace that serves red meat, I'll take it."

She nibbled her bottom lip, than finally said, "Do you consider pepperoni red meat? Because I could really go for some pizza."

He almost breathed a sigh of relief. Both that she'd said yes, and that she wasn't a woman who liked to nibble on a few carrots and pieces of lettuce and call it a meal.

"Perfect."

She managed a weak smile. "You say that a lot."

"You *are* that a lot."

He met her stare in the mirror. Amanda didn't exactly pull away at the gentle push into more personal, intimate territory that fell out of the boundaries of their sexy games. But the muscles beneath the silky skin tensed ever so slightly. Enough to warn him to back off.

He did. "Give me ten minutes to grab a shower."

Gently letting her go, he walked toward the bathroom, figuring she needed a chance to pull herself back together. Hell, so did he. Because in the past few minutes, it had hit him—hard—that despite being more intimate with the woman than he'd ever been with anyone in his life, he didn't know much about her.

Sure, he knew he liked her. Knew she had a great sense of humor, was smart and hardworking. Knew that right before she came, she emitted this adorable little high-pitched sound from the back of her throat.

Beyond that—not so much. He'd been to her place, in an old downtown Chicago highrise, but even seeing where she lived hadn't offered many answers about her personal life. She had no pets, no plants, no pictures, nothing that personalized her apartment at all. Entering it, he'd immediately known it was just a place for her to eat, sleep and chill—not really what anyone would call a home.

So maybe this time-out for dinner, with no play-acting, no innuendo…no sex…would be a good thing. Maybe it was time to take a step back, drop the pretense and actually get to know the real people playing the games.

She might not like it, she might not want it. But Reese did. Because he had the feeling the woman behind the wild seductress was someone he really wanted to get to know better.

As THEY WALKED INTO a nearby Italian restaurant recommended by the hotel's maitre d', Amanda found herself starting to sweat. And not just because Mr. Hotness was walking so closely behind her, his hand resting possessively on the small of her back.

This was too much like a date. Way too much like a date. And while she liked Reese Campbell a lot, dating him hadn't been part of the deal. Dating made this too real, when all she'd set out for from the beginning was a fantasy. A one-night stand that had somehow segued into two.

And only two. This was it, tonight *had* to be the end of it. Her life was just too complicated, and Reese was too incredible a guy for her to get any more involved with. He was too stable, too solid, too nice.

She...wasn't. Amanda wasn't dating material. She was sex material, oh, yes, she was good for flings and wild affairs, even if she'd had no time for any in recent months.

But dating? Romance? Relationships?

Uh-uh. She was the bitch who broke hearts. The one who panicked and took off whenever anybody got a little too serious or tried to tie her down in one place, instead of letting her live her life in flight, as she'd done for the past ten years.

This isn't a date. Just food so we can build up more energy to have lots more anonymous, no-strings sex.

"Would you relax?" Reese murmured as they followed the hostess, a fiftyish brunette in a full-skirted dress who'd yelled something in Italian as they passed by the swinging door to the kitchen. "It's just pizza, for God's sake."

Amanda drew in a long, shaky breath, trying to force the stiffness from her spine. Although, that was hard to do when his fingers were branding her.

"Is this all right?" the older woman asked as she reached a small, intimate table set for two.

"Just fine," Reese murmured.

Thank heaven he didn't say *perfect*. That word coming off his lips just had too many associations. Sometimes it made her incredibly horny, sometimes nervous as hell.

With its red-checked tablecloth, and an old Chianti bottle plugged with a candle and dripping wax, their table looked like the one where Lady and the Tramp had shared a romantic plate of spaghetti. All they needed was a pair of Italian singers with an accordion and a violin to serenade them.

God, this was *so* a date.

She almost bolted. If he hadn't already pulled out her chair and gently pushed her down into it, she probably would have done so.

It wouldn't have been the first time. One guy she'd been involved with had, despite all her warnings, told her he was in love with her. And she'd run to the airport, hopped on a flight to Paris and stayed away for two weeks.

No wonder he still drunk-dialed her.

But maybe this time could be different. Because he's different.

Reese was so different. So fun and sexy and playful. Daring and imaginative. He made her feel unlike any other man had before.

She sighed heavily, forcing those thoughts away. The way he made her feel couldn't possibly be a good thing. Not when it left her so confused, off-balance, unsure. Completely un-Amanda-like.

"Thank you," Reese said as he took the seat opposite her and smiled up at the hostess. Despite being at least twenty years his senior, she preened a little, as would any woman under the attention of a man as handsome as her companion.

Companion. Not date.

"So are you locals?" the woman asked.

Reese shook his head. "Just visiting."

"Excellent! Contrary to what you might think, Cleveland is a wonderful vacation spot. Very romantic," the woman said with a wag of her eyebrows. "Lots for a young couple in love to do."

Amanda opened her mouth to respond, lies and denials bubbling to her lips. They were just playing here…

just two wildly compatible people playing naughty games. Nothing more to it.

But before any could emerge, Reese reached for her hand and clasped it in his on top of the table. Their hostess nodded approvingly, then turned away to greet some newcomers standing in the entranceway.

"You were going to make up some outrageous story, weren't you?" he asked, casually releasing her hand, lifting a napkin and draping it over his lap.

"How do you know?"

"Are you denying it?"

"Of course not. Just wondering how you know."

"Oh, believe me, I'm starting to understand how your mind works. Romance, love…those words aren't in your vocabulary, right?"

She nodded once. "Right."

The hostess had left a basket of bread sticks on their table, and Amanda took one, nibbling lightly on the end, not elaborating even though she knew he probably expected her to. That kind of talk was for dates. This was just a…nutrition break.

"So what kind of story were you going to tell?" He sounded genuinely curious.

"I don't know." Thinking about it, she tapped her finger on her chin. "You're a witness against the mob in protective custody and I'm your bodyguard?"

"You're obviously not a very good bodyguard if you go around blabbing about me being a witness."

"I didn't say I was a good one. Maybe I'm a too-stupid-to-live one, like in one of those really bad movies."

"Hmm, possible." He looked around the restaurant, at the tables full of people who all looked much like their very-ethnic hostess, Rosalita. "But that might not be such a good idea in this place. I think half the diners in here are one generation out of Sicily. You might get me whacked."

"Got any better ideas?"

"Playboy bunny and mogul?"

"Keep dreaming." Giving him an impish look, she added, "Besides, I don't think you'd look very good in bunny ears."

He laughed out loud. Before he could reply, though, a busboy came over and filled two glasses of water, leaving them beside their untouched menus. A not-uncomfortable silence fell once the bored-looking teen had walked away.

Finally, Reese broke that silence. "So, why don't we just go with a pilot from Chicago hooking up with a businessman from Pittsburgh?"

She snorted, forcing herself to remain casual when her first reaction to the idea of just being who they really were more resembled panic. "Boring."

"You keep using that word…I do not think it means what you think it means."

Delighted that he'd quoted one of her favorite movies, *The Princess Bride,* complete with Spanish accent, she said, "Well done."

"Wow, we have something in common? A movie we've both seen?"

She gestured toward the table and the candle. "If we had the same taste in movies, you'd know just how ter-rified I am that some Italian dude is going to come up and start singing 'Bella Notte.'"

"At least tell me I'd get to be the Tramp in that one."

Something about his put-upon tone, plus the fact that

he knew exactly what she was talking about, made her relax and offer him her first genuine smile since they'd arrived. "I'm a pain in the ass, I know. I doubt you'd understand."

"I might. Why don't you try me?"

She thought about it. But how could she? How, exactly, did you go about telling your lover—*no, not lover, sex partner*—that you had a reputation as a bitch, that men faked suicide attempts because you couldn't love them, that you'd rather just not be bothered with the whole romance thing anymore? It wasn't exactly ladylike to admit you didn't want a guy who'd bring you chocolate and flowers and had long ago realized you were much more the fuck-buddy than the girlfriend type.

She couldn't say those things. And suddenly, she didn't want to. Not to him.

Why the very thought of it bothered her so much, though, she honestly didn't know.

When she didn't respond, he finally prompted, "Sometimes it's just easier to pretend than to be who you really are?"

"Yeah, something like that."

He shook his head ever so slightly, either disapproval or disappointment visible in the tightness of his mouth.

"Hey, you agreed to the terms."

"I agreed to a one-night stand." His eyes sparkled as he added, "You *changed* those terms with your e-mail."

He had a point.

"So maybe it's time to renegotiate."

Wary, she asked, "How so?"

"Maybe we should agree to at least one open, honest conversation, without any, uh, embellishments."

Figuring great sex would make him forget that idea, she licked her lips. "I don't see why you're complaining. I thought you were pretty happy about how things turned out this afternoon."

"As I recall, so were you. At least three times."

She licked the tip of her bread stick. "Mmm...six."

Reese crossed his arms over his chest and leaned back in his chair, eyeing her steadily. "I'm not counting the ones I wasn't involved in."

"Oh, honey, you were most definitely involved."

A brow arched over one blue eye. "Oh?"

"Mmm-hmm. And you've *been* involved every other time I've played with that little toy in the past two weeks."

He dropped his crossed arms onto the table, leaning over it, closer to her. Close enough that she saw the way his pulse pounded in his throat. "Is that so?"

"Yes."

He reached for his water, bringing the slick glass to his mouth. As he sipped, the muscles in his neck flexed. And when he lowered the glass, his lips were moist, parted. "Did that happen often?"

"Probably more than it had in the past year."

A masculine expression of self-satisfaction appeared on his incredibly handsome face. "You thought about..."

"Everything," she purred. "I thought about it a lot."

"Ditto."

She swallowed, immediately knowing what he was admitting. "I don't suppose you had any toys to play with?"

"'Fraid not. Had to go the old-fashioned route."

Squirming a little in her chair as she thought of him needing to gain some relief because he'd been thinking about her, she echoed his question. "Did that happen often?"

He lowered his eyes, gazing at her throat and the soft swell of cleavage rising above her V-necked sweater. "What do you think?"

Realizing she'd bit off a little more than she could chew, and that images of Reese pumping that long, thick shaft into his own tight fist were going to intrude on the rest of her meal, she cleared her throat and bit hard on the bread stick.

Reese didn't let it go, however, going right back to where he'd been headed before that detour into Lustville. "So what happened, your little toy was no longer enough so you decided to break your own rules and come back to order something else off the menu?"

She opened her mouth to answer, but before she could, a chirpy voice intruded. "Something else? Wait, has somebody already taken your order? Gosh darn it, I told her I was coming right over!"

Amanda bit her lip in amusement at the realization that a young waitress, whose name tag said Brittani, had overheard part of their conversation. Of course, she'd obviously misinterpreted it. Thank God.

The girl was probably only about seventeen, and she looked extremely annoyed that someone else had been poaching on her table. She apparently feared losing her tip. Considering they'd been left sitting here unattended for a good ten minutes, she was apparently the optimistic type.

"It's okay," Reese said, "we were talking about something else."

Amanda couldn't resist being a little mischievous. "Oh, yes. Definitely something else. Just reminiscing about something we ordered off a menu in Milan last week."

The girl's jaw opened far enough to display the chewing gum resting on her tongue. "You been to Australia? For real? Did you see any koala bears?"

Amanda managed to hide either a laugh or a sigh at Brittani's less-than-impressive geography skills.

"No koalas," Reese interjected smoothly. "Just a few dingoes. Now, if you don't mind, I think we're ready to order."

They did so, asking for the pepperoni pizza she'd been craving since they'd first talked about food back in the hotel room. Their perky waitress, whose mood had picked up once she realized nobody was horning in on her table, nodded and sauntered away, not even asking if they wanted anything other than ice water to drink.

The ice water that was just about gone.

When they were alone again, Reese said, "To be sure I've got it, let's clarify. Honest conversation is just as forbidden on your planet as actual dinner dates, right?"

Damn, the guy was tenacious. "Depends on the conversation."

"Can we talk about sports?"

She wrinkled her nose.

"Movies?"

"Sure. Though I haven't seen a new one in a theater in at least two years."

He shrugged. "Me, either. Moving on. Politics?"

"Only if you're a right-down-the-middle moderate like me."

"Progress. We have one thing in common."

Grinning impishly, she said, "I think we have more than one."

"Touché."

She lifted her glass and drained the last few drops of water from it, then sucked a small piece of ice into her mouth. "I think there's another thing we can safely agree on. Brittani's tip is getting smaller by the minute."

"I think we can also agree that world geography should be a required course in high schools."

She snickered, liking his deadpan sense of humor. Liking so much about him. Too much.

Maybe...

No. She wasn't going to go there, not even in her own head. She wasn't going to evaluate the possibility that this thing between them might be about anything more than having fun and incredible sex.

She'd take fun and incredible sex over angsty emotional dramas and minefields of feelings any day.

Despite her best efforts, for a few minutes Amanda let herself actually converse with the man. Nothing too heavy, definitely no sharing of past relationships or deepest fears. He got her to admit she'd once had a mad crush on every member of the Backstreet Boys, and he'd come clean about his secret desire to be a drummer for a rock band, even though he'd never held a drumstick.

"Backstreet Boys never had a drummer," she pointed out.

"Too bad. To think we could have started all this fun fifteen years ago."

"Fifteen years ago, we would both have been seriously underage."

"But think of all the interesting things we could have learned together."

Frankly, she was learning lots of interesting things from the man, right here and now. At fourteen, still the rebel trying to survive in good-girl wonderland, she didn't think her heart could have taken meeting someone who excited her like Reese Campbell.

Well, her heart probably could have. Her parents, however, would have lost their minds.

Their light chatting seemed to satisfy Reese, at least for now, and he didn't try to steer her toward any more personal subjects. That was fortunate. Amanda honestly didn't know if she'd have been able to explain her aversion to such things. Not without giving him all the information he was looking for in the process. Her past heartbreaks, her rigid upbringing, her bad reputation for being a little too footloose and coldhearted…all explained who she was today. But none were topics she particularly cared to talk about. Teenage fantasy was about as intimate as she wanted to get.

"Okay, here you go. Enjoy!"

Brittani had returned with their pizza right on time—before Reese could slip through any conversational back doors she might have inadvertently left open. She was so anxious that it remain that way, she grabbed a slice and bit into it right away.

Bad move.

"Ow!" she snapped when the gooey cheese burned the roof of her mouth.

Reese immediately scooped a piece of ice out of his own water glass and lifted it toward her. Dropping the pizza, Amanda gratefully parted her lips, sucking the cube he offered into her mouth. Her tongue swiped across his fingertips as she did so, and suddenly the pain wasn't so bad. Seeing the way his eyes flared at the brush of her tongue against his skin, she had to acknowledge it wasn't so bad at all.

"Watch it. Don't want any injuries that could cut short our two-night stand," he teased. Then, looking at his own pizza, he added, "I think I'll wait a while for this to cool off. I have definite plans for my mouth tonight."

She quivered in her seat at the very thought of it. Because oh, the man did know how to use his mouth. And there were such wonderful things he could do with it that did not involve the conversation she suspected he would want to get back to as soon as they finished eating.

She thought about it. Stick around here and deal with lots more talking? Or just seduce the man back to their hotel room?

No-freaking-brainer.

"Reese?" she said, speaking carefully, the ice now just a small sliver on her tongue.

"Yeah?"

"Can we please take this to go?"

He stared at her, as if gauging the request, and her motivation for making it. She didn't have to feign her interest in getting back to where they'd been a couple of hours ago: in a hotel room bed. But she did have to hide the fact that her motivation was at least partly to get out of having to talk anymore.

Something that looked like understanding crossed his face, though she would swear she saw a hint of frustration there, too. "You're sure?"

"I think you need to kiss this better," she said, pushing him just a little more. She swiped her tongue across her lips to punctuate the point.

He shook his head, smiling ruefully. "I guess I should be thankful just to have found out you're a political moderate who doesn't go to the movies. That's more than I knew two hours ago."

"And don't forget—not a sports fan."

"We're really getting somewhere."

"Now let's get somewhere else," she insisted, leaning across the table. This back-and-forth conversation was reminding her of how much she liked his quick wit, his easygoing personality. Physically, she'd been attracted from the get-go. Now she knew there was so much more about him that interested her.

But only until tomorrow.

Unless…

Only until tomorrow!

"Please," she whispered. "We only have until morning and I really don't want to waste it sitting here waiting for the pizza to cool off."

Apparently hearing her sincerity, he no longer hesitated. He waved to their waitress, then murmured, "But I do reserve the right to ask you if you've read any good books lately on the ride back to the hotel."

"Books. Okay, I can do that."

And she could. Books were fine. So were movies and politics and sports and anything else that didn't really require intimate conversation.

He just couldn't ask her about her past relationships, her family background or her footloose lifestyle. She wouldn't share details of her aversion to small towns, home, hearth, wholesome values or anything else resembling the world in which she'd grown up.

And she definitely didn't want to talk about her slightly hardened heart. Or the fact that some people didn't even seem to think she had one.

5

Thanksgiving

"So, I've been meaning to ask you, how'd your folks take you not coming home for the holiday weekend?"

Sprawled back in a comfortable, cushy chair in the rec room of her friend Jazz's parents' house, Amanda resisted the urge to unsnap her khakis. After the two full plates of Thanksgiving dinner, plus the pumpkin pie and the teensy sliver of pecan that she'd simply had to taste, she should be glad the snap hadn't just popped on its own.

"Manda? Were they upset?"

Tryptophan kicking in, she yawned and shook her head. "Actually, I think they were relieved."

Jazz, who supervised the mechanics who kept Clear-Blue Air flying, curled up in her own chair, her head barely reaching the top of it. She was petite, five-foot-four, but you'd never know that by the way she ran her mechanics' shop or the magic way she coaxed the best performance out of an airplane.

The two of them were hiding down in the converted basement. They'd finished dinner a few hours ago and

Jazz's big family had just begun saying their goodbyes. Neither of them being the air-kisses type, Amanda and Jazz were waiting out the big huggy scene downstairs. Once the coast was clear, they would go back up and let Jazz's mother make a big fuss out of loading up plates of leftovers for the "single girls" to take home.

It was becoming a tradition. Somehow, hanging out with Jazz's big, loud, crazy family on holidays was easier than going home and sticking out like a sore thumb in her own small, quiet, proper one.

"Relieved why?"

"You know Abby got engaged?"

Jazz nodded with a big roll of her dark eyes. She'd met Amanda's younger sister last year when Abby had come to the city for a spring shopping trip.

Abby was okay, at least when their parents weren't around and she didn't have to play Miss Perfect. But the stick up her ass only ever came out so far, and Jazz was not the type around whom Abigail Bauer would ever let down her guard.

Jazz was an exotically beautiful, loud-mouthed, crass, wild-child. Abby was a demure, classically beautiful, prodigal one. Oil and water.

Which made Amanda, what…the vinegar to their Good Seasons salad dressing?

Yeah, tart and sour.

She thrust that thought away, preferring to think of herself as flavorful and zesty.

"How do you like her fiancé?"

"He's a douche."

Back to tart and sour.

Jazz snorted, sipping from the glass of wine she'd smuggled down from the kitchen. "Figures."

"He's as cold as my father and as reserved as my mother. And he comes from a family of people just like him. His parents invited my folks over for a prewedding holiday meal today."

"Gotcha. No bad girls allowed, huh?"

Amanda lifted a brow, feigning offense. "Look who's talking."

Jazz bent her head and smiled into her glass. "I'm not the one flying off tomorrow to have a weekend of illicit sex with a guy I barely know."

Sucking her bottom lip between her teeth, Amanda reached for her glass of water. Because damn it, yes, she was doing exactly that.

She'd left Cleveland absolutely certain she'd never see Reese Campbell again. She'd felt sure she'd gotten him out of her system. They'd had a great time, built some incredible memories. Plus they'd done just about everything two people could do together sexually.

Okay, that was a lie. She could think of about another four or five things she'd like to do with the man. Or five dozen.

The point was, they'd had amazing sexual encounters twice now, and twice was once more than the one-night stand she'd intended. So how crazy was she to go for number three?

Third time's the charm.

She'd been unable to resist. Hearing his voice on her voice mail the other day, she'd gotten shaky and weak all over again. When he'd asked her if she wanted to meet him in Florida to see if they could get kicked out of a theme park for having hot sex in public, she'd been unable to say anything but yes. She hadn't even insisted that he promise to put on any mouse ears.

She had something else in mind for the fantasy part of their sensual weekend. Something a little more risqué than a theme park.

"Where are you meeting him?"

"Daytona."

"Warm. Sounds good. So, uh, when are you going to let me meet this guy?"

"Never."

Her friend pulled a hurt look. "Come on, I introduce you to all my boy toys."

"He's not my boy toy. He's…"

"He's what?" Jazz asked, leaning forward and dropping her elbows onto her knees.

Good question. She couldn't really call Reese a stranger anymore. They not only knew and had explored every inch of each other's bodies, they'd also spent time together doing nonsexual things. Damn it, she'd gotten roped into pillow talk that last time.

Even worse, they'd actually chatted about his family the morning after. Mainly because his teenage sister had called him at the butt-crack of dawn to ask him to intervene with their mother for permission to go to some party.

Even adorably tousled and sleepy, Reese had been kind and patient with the girl, whose loud voice Amanda could hear from the other side of the bed. She'd watched him during the conversation, seeing the great guy, the caring brother.

He'd told her a little about his family after the call. That his father had died, that he'd taken over as head of the family business. He hadn't had to tell her he'd taken on his father's role in his younger siblings' lives, too. She'd heard it in the tender—and a little over-whelmed—tone when he talked about them.

Those were about a half-dozen more details than she had ever intended to learn about him. Especially because every one of them just made him that much more appealing.

She absolutely should have steered well clear after that. So how dumb was she to have said yes to this weekend's get-together? Extremely. And yet, she was already almost breathless with excitement when she thought about the fact that she'd be with him again in under twenty-four hours.

"I guess he's just a pretty big distraction right at the moment," she finally admitted.

"I'm glad," Jazz declared. "It's about damn time."

"I know. Now I don't have to give up my membership card to the sexually alive club."

"I don't mean that." Jazz finished off her wine, then got up and crossed to a well-stocked bar, digging around in a fridge for another bottle. She held it up questioningly, but Amanda shook her head. She'd had one glass with dinner. That was her max, considering she was flying the next day.

"So what did you mean?" Amanda asked, once her friend returned to her seat.

"I mean, it's about time you stop thinking about what that creepazoid Dale said to you when you dumped his sorry ass. You're not cold, you're not ruthless and you're no heartbreaker."

Amanda couldn't help humming a few bars of the Pat Benatar song under her breath.

Jazz ignored her. "He was a tool."

True.

"And that fake-overdose shit also proved he was one taco short of a combination plate."

Also true. But he wasn't the only man she'd ever let down. Something her loyal friend was apparently trying to ignore.

"Face it," Amanda said, "moss doesn't grow under my feet. In thirty years, I'm going to be like Uncle Frank. I'll be the one flying off to the Bahamas to hook up with some hot divorcée for the Thanksgiving holiday."

Hell, she was already like Uncle Frank. Suddenly, she wished she could have that second glass of wine.

"If you're swinging that way in thirty years, I might just have to be the hot divorcée."

Amanda snorted with laughter, as Jazz had obviously intended her to. Because the girl was about as flaming a heterosexual as she'd ever known. Jazz often said her favorite color was purple-veined penis.

"Give yourself a chance," Jazz murmured, her smile fading and her tone turning earnest. "Don't decide what this is before you have the opportunity to really find out."

Amanda opened her mouth to respond, but didn't quite know what to say. So she said nothing and simply nodded.

They fell silent for a minute or two. Then, from upstairs, they heard the tromping of feet and the slam of the back door, which meant that Jazz's mother was ushering out the rest of her guests. They'd managed to successfully avoid the big so-great-to-see-you-let's-do-this-more-often goodbye. The two of them lifted their glasses in a silent toast.

To hiding out when the going gets tough, and avoiding emotional entanglements.

She just had to keep reminding herself of that thought for the next couple of days. And not think about the silent promise she'd just made to her best friend.

AS HE DROVE HIS RENTAL CAR closer to the beachfront hotel where Amanda awaited him, Reese had sex on his mind. Wild sex. Steamy sex. Crazy, never-thought-it-could-be-this-good sex.

That had been on his mind for days. Ever since he'd driven away from that Cleveland hotel room, unsure of whether he would ever again see the beautiful woman who'd slept in his arms the night before.

This time, he'd played it a little smarter. He hadn't called or e-mailed her right away. Despite how much it killed him, he'd let a full of week go by before he'd tried to contact her.

And it had paid off. Amanda had let her guard down enough to admit she missed him and wanted to see him again. She'd agreed that Thanksgiving weekend in Florida sounded like a perfect holiday.

He should have known it wouldn't stay entirely perfect. Nothing ever did, right?

"Damn it," he muttered, seeing a blue light come on behind him, and hearing the brief trill of a siren.

He was a good driver. But when it came to these getaways with the most exciting woman he'd ever known, even his foot got excited and pressed down a bit too hard on the gas pedal.

He could see their hotel, an older place with a sign showing a blue dolphin leaping through the waves. The thought that Amanda was waiting behind the door of one of the rooms, while he was going to have to spend the next fifteen or twenty minutes just a few yards away dealing with a ticket was frustrating in the extreme.

He put the car's emergency flashers on and pulled into the hotel parking lot, praying the cop was in a good holiday mood. Considering it was Black Friday, however, and he'd probably been chasing credit-card-crazy shoppers clamoring to make it from door-buster to door-buster, Reese somehow doubted he'd be that lucky.

The cop who'd pulled him over spoke from a few feet away as Reese lowered the window. "License and registration?"

Reese started at the female voice, glancing over and seeing the shapely woman standing beside the car door. She was dressed in a formfitting uniform, and wore dark sunglasses even though it was just after sunset. She stared down at him, not taking them off.

"Good evening, Officer," he said slowly. "Is there some kind of problem?"

"You were doing forty in a twenty-five."

"Really? Are you sure about that?"

She bent down into the open window. "You saying I'm wrong?"

"Not wrong. Just maybe…mistaken?"

"You have a smart mouth. Maybe I should haul you in."

He offered her his most charming smile. "I'd really appreciate it if you didn't. I've got a busy night planned."

She fisted her hands and put them on her shapely hips. "You think your night's more important than the safety of everyone else on the road?"

He hesitated, giving it some thought.

"Step out of the car," she snapped.

Reese didn't argue but did as she ordered. Removing

the keys from the ignition, he opened the door and stepped out into the thick Florida night. Despite the fact that it was November, heat assaulted him. Though it was already evening, the air was still heavy and hot, with that not unpleasant smell found only in the south. A mixture of citrus, flowers, paper mills and suntan oil.

And spicy, sultry female cop.

"Don't you think we could come to some kind of arrangement, Officer? Can't you get me off…excuse me, I mean, let me off, with a warning or something?"

Her lips tightened. "I don't think a warning will do."

He lifted both his hands, palms up. "There must be some kind of arrangement we could reach. Something I could do for you so you'd feel comfortable forgetting about my speeding?"

She rubbed her hand on her slim jaw, her lips pursed. Then, as if she'd come to some decision, she slowly nodded.

"Okay, then. Maybe you can sweet-talk me into not writing you a ticket."

"Talk?" he asked, moving closer, until the tips of his shoes touched hers and the fabric of their pants brushed. "You sure that's all you want from me? Conversation?"

She swallowed visibly, her throat moving with the effort. Reese lifted his hand, tracing the tip of his index finger from her full bottom lip, down her chin, then her throat, her neck. All the way to the top button of her blouse.

This time, her hard swallow was preceded by a shaky sigh.

"Which room?" he asked, urgency making his voice weak.

She lifted a shaky hand and pointed to the nearest one, on the end.

"Key?"

Tugging it out of her pocket, she handed the key card to him, then put her hand in his and let him lead her across the parking lot. Just before he opened the door, he glanced back at the car, and the motor scooter—obviously a beachside rental—sitting directly behind it.

Smirking, he said, "Not even a real motorcycle? It's not terribly intimidating."

"Maybe not," she said with a wicked smile. Then she reached into her pocket and pulled out something… something metal. Something that jangled. "But these are definitely real."

Handcuffs. Oh, yeah. They were real. And they were most definitely intimidating.

He just wondered what his sexy-lover-playing-cop was going to say when he got the upper hand and used them on *her*. She might think she was in charge this time, but she'd played that role in Cleveland. It was his turn.

"Okay, Officer Bauer. I guess I'm your prisoner."

At least for a few minutes. As soon as he could gain the upper hand, he'd be the one calling the shots, leaving her vulnerable and helpless against every bit of pleasure he could possibly give her.

AMANDA DIDN'T KNOW WHAT happened. One second, Reese was lying on the bed, his shirt off, pants unfastened, arms upstretched toward the headboard. The next, *she* was flat on her back and wearing one of the sets of handcuffs.

She sputtered. "What are you doing?"

He didn't answer at first, too busy double-checking the cuffs that attached her left hand to the headboard. The other set was lying on the bed, but instead of reaching for it, he hesitated. "We don't have to use both…if you're not comfortable."

She had fully intended to use both sets on him, wanting him totally at her mercy. How wonderful Reese was to take it just far enough, but then pause to make sure she was okay with what he was doing.

Not a lot of men would do that. Of course, not a lot of women would say 'to hell with it' and offer up her other wrist for restraint, either.

But they weren't exactly your average couple.

"Go for it," she said with a sultry smile as she twisted on the sheets, suddenly so aroused she could barely stand it.

He reached across the bed, fastening her other hand, then came back to center, brushing his mouth against hers.

"I've wanted you since the last time I saw you," she told him.

"I know."

He wasn't being arrogant, she realized. He knew because he felt the same way.

"Okay, you've got me, big guy. Now what are you going to do?"

Reese had been almost undressed when she tried to take over, but Amanda hadn't removed so much as her shoes. Which would probably present a bit of a problem when it came to her top. But she trusted him—he was a very resourceful kind of guy.

And it buttoned up the front. Thankfully.

"I'll think of something." He frowned down at her. "So, madam police officer, are you used to trading sexual favors for legal ones?"

"Only in very special circumstances."

He rose to his knees, reaching for her waistband, and unfastened her pants. Amanda lifted up a little so he could slide them down over her hips and bottom, feeling the slow glide of his fingertips down to her very bones.

"What circumstances would those be?"

"Well, when I haven't had a man in a very long time." She licked her lips. "And I stumble across one who looks like he could satisfy me."

He tsked. "Didn't we have this conversation in a beer closet once? Is there any doubt that I can satisfy you?"

Giving him an innocent look, she asked, "A beer closet? Why, I don't know what you mean."

He reached for her tiny panties, catching the elastic and pulling them off the way he had her pants. This time, she didn't help. She let him work them down, liking the way he couldn't take his eyes off her body as he revealed it.

Those blue eyes darkened as he stared at her hips, her pelvis, the curls at the top of her sex. But he didn't touch, seeming content to drive her mad with just a stare.

He could set out to be as slow and deliberate as he wanted. Amanda knew, however, that his strength would only last so long.

She'd been there, done that, and brought home the orgasms to prove it.

Bare from the waist down, she casually lifted one leg, letting her thighs fall apart so he could see the glistening effect he'd already had on her.

He hesitated for a second, then, as if unable to resist, he reached for her. Tracing her pelvic bone with his fingertips, he finally slid them down to swirl over her clit.

Amanda jerked, her hips lifting off the bed. He didn't go any faster, or further, he just continued to toy with her, to pluck her like a fine instrument, until she was gasping. Then he moved his hand away and reached for the bottom button of her blouse. He unfastened it, pressing his mouth to the bare skin of her belly. The next button—and that wicked, wonderful mouth moved higher.

By the time he reached her midriff, his tongue was involved and he was taking tiny tastes of her, as if he was nibbling delicately on some luscious dessert. She twisted beneath him, arching toward that questing mouth and those careful fingers.

For the first time, she got a sense of just how difficult this being restrained was going to be. Because she desperately wanted to twine her hands in his hair, to caress his handsome face, cup his strong jaw.

She also wanted to pull him up a teensy bit faster. Her breasts were throbbing with need, her nipples scraping almost painfully against the rough, starched blouse— part of her phony uniform. And having his mouth on her skin, his breaths blowing hotly against her, all she could think about was how incredible his tongue felt on other parts of her anatomy.

But she could do nothing: couldn't hurry him, couldn't

touch herself to provide some relief. She could only lie there, silently begging with every quiver of her body.

"What's wrong?" he asked, and there was laughter in his voice.

She faked it. "Not a thing."

"Uh-huh. Sure."

He moved up again. One inch closer to where she needed him to be. Or one inch farther from where she needed him to be. She honestly couldn't decide.

Well, of course she could. She wanted both. Wanted him sucking her nipples and also giving her the kind of mind-blowing oral sex that she'd had erotic dreams about for weeks.

"Please…"

He moved again, this time his slightly roughened cheek scraping the bottom curve of her breast. His lips followed, kissing away the irritation, and she flinched with the close contact to her sensitized nipples.

Finally the right button. He looked down on her and shook his head. "No bra? Is that standard uniform attire, Officer?"

She twisted, trying to push her nipple toward his mouth, needing him to suck and squeeze and twist.

"Your breasts are a work of art," he mumbled, dropping his aloof act.

She didn't totally agree, always feeling at least a cup size less adequate than most women. But they were pretty, nicely shaped and high. Plus her nipples had so many nerve endings it was a wonder she didn't come when she wore a silk blouse.

"Suck me, Reese," she begged.

"That an order?" He pulled farther away, deliberately tormenting her.

"Let's call it a polite request."

"Well, since you're being polite."

He said nothing else, gave her no warning, merely bent to capture the taut tip between his lips. He sucked her once, then deeper, reaching up to catch the other mound in his hand.

She cried out, her hips instinctively jerking toward his jean-covered legs. Twisting her thigh over his, she tugged him closer, gaining satisfaction from the brush of his jeans against her sex.

She was all nerve endings, all sensation, and between the deep, strong pulls of his mouth on her nipple and the rub of his strong, masculine thigh between her legs, she felt herself begin to climax. The wave began, and she let out a hitchy little cry.

Reese moved suddenly, removing all that physical connection. He covered her mouth with his, swallowing down the sound with a kiss. And the orgasm dissipated like morning fog baked away by the rising sun.

"Not yet," he whispered. "Not just yet."

Oh, God. She was going to kill him. "Paybacks are hell," she snapped.

"Yeah, I know." He moved his mouth to her neck, sucking her skin into his mouth and biting her lightly. "Consider this a payback for November 11th."

Oh. Yeah. The day she'd kept him on the brink of climax but hadn't let him go over the edge until she was good and ready.

"Can I just cry uncle, say you win and take my orgasm now, please?"

"Nope."

Damn. She'd been afraid of that.

Reese was as good as his word. For the next hour,

he tormented her, delighted her, toyed with her, thrilled her. There was magic in the man's hands and heaven in his mouth. And he used those hands and that mouth on every last inch of her.

Her shoulders became sore from twisting around on the bed while her arms were restrained above her head. But, to be honest, Amanda didn't mind. There was something incredibly freeing about being at the sexual mercy of someone she trusted completely. There was no quid pro quo, no reciprocity. She just had to lie there and let him give her pleasure, just take, take, take and not feel one bit of guilt about it.

It wasn't until she was sobbing with the need to come that Reese finally decided to grant her an orgasm. He'd been moving his mouth and tongue across her groin, her upper thighs and the outer lips of her sex, but not lingering long enough. Finally, though, perhaps hearing the sobs of pleasure mingled with frustration, he did linger.

Oh, did he linger.

Swirling his tongue over her clit, he flicked and sucked, then upped the intensity by moving a hand to her swollen lips. He wet his finger in her body's moisture, then slid it into her. Then another, moving slowly, deeply.

"Oh, yes," she said. "More, please."

He gave her more. More pressure, more suction, more delicate stabs of his tongue. And he began to withdraw his fingers, then plunge them in again, filling her as best he could until he could use the part of his anatomy she really wanted.

"Oh, God, finally!" she cried as the waves of pleasure erupted. Nothing could have held them back this time.

Her body had reached its very peak of sexual arousal and the explosion that rocked her seemed to last for a solid minute. She almost had an out-of-body experience, she was so in its grip.

By the time it finally released her, she realized Reese had moved away long enough to strip out of his clothes. His erection was enormous, looking bigger somehow, as if seeing her so entirely lost had aroused him more than he'd ever been before.

He paused only long enough to pull on a condom, then moved between her splayed thighs. Amanda immediately tilted up to greet him, wrapping her legs around his hips, wanting him as deep as he could possibly get.

They knew each other now. Knew what they wanted, what they liked, what they could take. So there was nothing tentative, no gentle easing like there'd been the first time, when he'd almost seemed worried he might hurt her.

This time, Reese drove into her in one thrust. Though she was dripping wet and took him easily, Amanda let out a little scream of pleasure. He filled her thoroughly, stretching out a place for himself, making her wonder how she withstood the emptiness when he wasn't inside her.

She wanted her hands free, wanted to wrap them around his neck and hold on tight. But he was too hungry for her to consider asking him to pause to find the keys.

Oh, what the hell.

Amanda didn't even think about it. She easily slid her hand out of the left cuff, twisted the right and tugged that one free, too. Reese had been so tender and sweet about it, not wanting to hurt her, that he hadn't fastened the damn things tightly enough.

His eyes flared in surprise when she lifted her hands to his thick, broad shoulders. "Sneaky woman."

"You don't have to be gentle," she told him, not just referring to the cuffs.

"I know." His eyes glittered as he withdrew, then slammed back into her, hard, deep, almost violent.

Nothing had ever felt so good. Nothing. Not ever.

Amanda raked her nails across his back. Wanting even more, she tilted farther until her legs were so high, he took them and looped them over his shoulders.

"Yes, yes...."

Smiling down at her, Reese bent to catch her mouth in another hungry kiss. His warm tongue thrust deeply against hers, catching the rhythm of his thick member moving in and out of her body. She matched both movements, taking everything, giving it back again. Until finally, in a lot shorter time than he'd allowed for hers, he came close to reaching his own ultimate level of fulfillment. She knew, by his hoarse groans and the strain on his face, that he was almost there.

Not willing to be left behind, yet not wanting to give up one centimeter of that deep possession, she reached down between their bodies, rubbing at her most sensitive spot with her fingertips. Reese looked down, and she followed his stare. It was incredibly erotic, seeing her fingers tangled in her curls, and below, his big, thick cock disappearing into her.

The sights, the sounds, the weight of him, the smell of him, and, oh, the feel of his body joined with hers... all combined to drive her up to that ledge again. And once he saw she was right there with him, Reese brought them both as high as they could possibly go…and then just a little bit further.

THOUGH THEIR PREVIOUS encounters had, literally, been one-nighters, this trip to Daytona was actually going to last two. Amanda had booked the hotel room through Sunday, and Reese wasn't about to ask her why. She again wanted to change the terms of their…whatever it was. Well, that was just fine with him. Double the pleasure, double the fun.

Problem was, by Saturday afternoon, he could see she was beginning to regret it. Her smiles were forced. She kept averting her gaze during their brief talks. And whenever he began any kind of real conversation, she tried to seduce him.

Not that he minded being seduced. Seriously. But he was only human and while the mind was willing, his dick was just about worn-out after six or seven rounds of cops and robbers.

Amanda had even resisted going out to eat, having filled the small fridge with food before his arrival. He knew without asking that she was remembering their dinner at the Italian place in Cleveland. Her aversion to anything that looked, smelled or sounded anything like a date had come through loud and clear. He didn't know why she felt that way—how could he?—but the message had definitely been received.

Still, he'd had enough of grapes and cheese. Not to mention enough of her skittishness about doing anything that didn't involve some part of his anatomy connecting with some part of hers. And that was why, at three o'clock Saturday, he put his foot down, insisting they get out of the hotel room and actually see the ocean they could hear pounding right outside their window.

"I didn't bring a bathing suit," she muttered as he nudged her toward the door.

"I didn't, either. The water's not exactly swimming temperature, is it?" Though, judging by the clear blue sky and blazing yellow sun he could sort-of see through the tired, smudged windows, he figured it had to be as hot as a typical summer day in Pittsburgh. "A walk on the beach doesn't require special clothing. And I might be lucky enough to find a hot dog vendor or something. Because if I have to eat nothing but cheddar cheese for the rest of the day, I'm going to fly to Vermont and shoot someone."

Though a grin pulled at her mouth, she visibly subdued it. With her brow tugged down, she looked like someone trying to get out of some difficult chore. "Fine. We'll walk."

"You know, if I hadn't already seen just how daring you can be, I'd have to conclude you were a total chickenshit."

Her eyes flared wide in surprise. "What did you call me?"

"You heard me," he said with a shrug.

"I'm not afraid of the beach," she insisted.

He'd lay money she intentionally misunderstood. "I didn't say you were."

"Then what are you saying?"

Putting a hand on her elbow, he led her out the door while she was distracted being all pissed off. "I'm just wondering something. Are you scared that if you take your hands out of my pants for too long, you might actually start to like me?"

Her face flushed, but, as he'd figured, she kept on walking, now challenged more than anything else.

It took a full minute for her to respond. As they crossed the wooden planking over the dunes and stepped down onto the sandy beach, she finally muttered, "I don't dislike you."

"Progress."

She fell silent again while they stopped to kick off their shoes. As he'd suspected, it was blazingly hot out, at least fifty degrees warmer than it had been yesterday in Pittsburgh. While he definitely could appreciate the warmth, he honestly didn't think he'd ever actually enjoy living someplace like this. Wearing shorts while watching football on Thanksgiving day just sounded wrong on all kinds of levels.

Carrying their shoes, they made their way down toward the water. They skirted the pasty-skinned sunbathers, on vacation from cold northern cities, who were sprawled on colorful towels and slathered with lotion. Only when the warm ocean surf lapped at their feet did they turn and proceed north.

Heading away from the hotels, the beach grew less and less crowded. Soon the voices of shouting kids, radios and gabby teenagers had disappeared. There was nothing but the churning of the waves, the hiss of the breeze and the squawk of overhead seagulls. And the very loud silence of his companion.

It was probably a good ten minutes before Amanda said a thing. When she did, it was in a whisper he could barely hear above the strong lapping of the surf against his ankles.

"I actually like you a lot, Reese."

He said nothing, just reached for her hand and laced

his fingers through hers. He'd touched her in so many ways, but this was, as far as he could recall, the first time he'd simply held her hand.

Amanda had such a strong, confident personality, he sometimes forgot how feminine she was. Her slender hand, delicate fingers and soft palm reminded him that, despite the swagger and the attitude, she was still vulnerable. More than she'd ever want anyone to realize.

"I probably like you too much already." She sounded as though she'd just admitted to liking tuna-and-peanut-butter sandwiches.

"I wish I could say I understand why that's such a bad thing."

"I told you I didn't want anything serious."

"Who said liking each other meant we were about to exchange rings?"

She stopped, but didn't pull her hand away. Tilting her head back to look up at him, she pushed her sunglasses up onto the top of her thick hair, as if wanting to ensure he understood what she was about to say. He did the same, seeing confusion in her green eyes.

"Here's the thing. I am poison when it comes to men and relationships. My name might as well be Ivy."

He didn't laugh, knowing she was dead serious. She really believed what she said. "Why do you think that?"

"Because I've been *told* that. I break hearts and hurt people, Reese."

"Intentionally?"

Her brow furrowing in confusion, she shook her head slowly. "No, I suppose not. But what difference does that make?"

Leaning down, he pressed his lips onto her forehead,

kissing her tenderly. There was nothing sexual in it, just warmth and a bit of consolation for this beautiful woman who seemed to see herself so differently than the way he saw her.

"It makes all the difference in the world," he murmured.

She remained stiff, unyielding. "Not to the guys whose hearts I've broken."

"Armies of them, I suppose?"

She wasn't teased out of her dark mood.

"Platoons?" Reese put his arms around her shoulders, tugging her against him, making her take the support and connection she tried so hard to resist. "Squads?"

"I don't know how big those things are," she mumbled into his shirt, her voice sounding a little watery.

He didn't tease her, didn't pull back to see if those really were tears dampening the front of his shirt or just the misty spray off the ocean.

"I don't, either. And I honestly don't care."

He meant it. He was a grown man, and she'd warned him from the get-go. He could take care of himself.

He only wondered if she was really as tough as she tried to make herself out to be, or if all these protestations and fears were more about protecting her own heart than anyone else's. Not that he was about to say that out loud. Not when she had, at last, seemed to let down her guard, at least a little bit.

"Let's just go with this—no more rules, no more walls. And see where it takes us. Okay?"

No answer. Instead, quietly, slowly, she relaxed against him. After a few moments, she even slid her arms around his waist, holding him, if not tightly, at least comfortably.

They stood that way for a long while, on the edge of the water, with the waves splashing against their legs. And in the quiet stillness of the moment, he felt the tension leave her, felt her give up some of the control she'd been trying so very hard to maintain.

And finally she murmured, "Okay."

He didn't respond or react in any way, knowing the decision had been a difficult one for her to make. He also knew they'd just agreed to something that could end up not working at all.

Because what was happening between them was unpredictable, as uncontrollable as the currents sending the salty ocean water splashing over their feet. He didn't know where they were going or how long it would take to get there. Or how long they'd stay.

He was just glad Amanda had finally appeared to decide to continue the journey with him.

6

December 7

SEEING THE NUMBER ON HER caller ID as it rang very late one weeknight, Amanda almost didn't answer the phone. Not because she didn't want to talk to Reese, but because she *did* want to...a little too much.

They hadn't spoken since they'd parted at the airport the Sunday after Thanksgiving. Yes, they'd exchanged a few e-mails, but neither of them had pushed it, both realizing things had changed during their walk on the beach.

Amanda hadn't yet decided how she felt about that change. Going from a holiday fling to a long-distance relationship was such a big step. An enormous one, at least for her. So the cooling-off period had seemed like a very good idea. Mentally, she'd been hoping her common sense would slowly edge out her libido and she'd somehow find the strength to tell him she had changed her mind and it was over.

Not seeing him again was the best course of action. They hadn't gone too far yet. At this point, he couldn't decide to hate her and blame her for leading him on.

Couldn't accuse her of taking his heart and crushing it beneath the heel of her boots when she left.

Logically, she knew all that. But as the days had dragged on, she'd begun to realize how much she missed him. She missed *everything* about him. She wanted to hear the laughter in his voice, and the sexy way he said her name. She missed the whispers about how much he wanted her when they made love. She even found herself missing the way he kept trying to get her to talk about her past, her family and her lousy romantic track record.

She missed his touch.

Third ring. Fourth. She swallowed hard, twisting in her bed, the covers tangling around her legs. Her muscles flexed, the blood rushing a just bit harder through her veins. Her senses perked up, the scratch of the sheets on her bare skin, the image of his face, the thought of his hands and his mouth.

She hadn't reached for her little sex toy in a few weeks, and if she answered the phone, she had the feeling she would need it. Hearing his voice, wanting him but not having him, would take the low, edgy need throbbing deep inside her and push it up like lava rising in a volcano.

Of course, not answering would still leave her needing it. So she might as well enjoy it. "Hello?"

"Do you realize that today is National Cotton Candy Day?"

She chuckled, wondering how the man could amuse her when she was suddenly so damned horny. "Funny, I had figured you were calling because it's Pearl Harbor Day." She had half thought about it herself, sticking to their holiday theme.

"That's too somber," he said. "Cotton candy's a lot more cheerful. It's very pink."

"I'm not a pink kinda girl."

He didn't even pause. "It can also be blue."

"An expert at cotton candy, are you?"

"Let's just say I'd like to become better acquainted with it. Especially with what I'm picturing right now."

She settled deeper into the pillow, the phone nestled in the crook of her neck. "What are you picturing?"

"You. Wearing nothing but a lot of fluffy cotton candy."

Laughing softly, she said, "Sounds sticky."

"Sounds delicious."

"You really think you could eat that much?"

"I could dine on you for days, Amanda Bauer."

Okay, definitely gonna need the vibrator tonight. Sighing in utter pleasure at the sound of his need for her, she kicked the covers totally off. She bent one knee, letting her legs fall apart, barely noticing the cold night air. The heat of his whispers warmed her enough.

"Where are you?" he asked, his voice thick, as if he'd suddenly realized she was no longer thinking light and flirty thoughts, but deep and sultry ones.

"I'm in my great big bed, all by my lonesome."

"Mmm. And what are you wearing."

"Not a blessed thing."

"Hold it…ahh, now you are. I see you. All wrapped in blue fluff just waiting for me to eat it off you."

Amanda licked her lips, then slid her hand across her stomach, tracing her fingertips along the bottom curves of her breasts. "Where are you?" she asked.

"In bed. Of course, I don't have as much privacy. I'm not alone like you are."

She stiffened, though realistically she knew he wouldn't be calling if he had a woman with him. Especially because he knew if he did, she'd fly to Pittsburgh and punch him.

"Get down, Ralph."

Hearing a low woof in the background, she realized who he was talking about. "Ahh. Your dog."

"Out you go, buddy," he said. She heard the click of a door as the dog apparently got sent out of the bedroom for the night. Then Reese admitted, "He's not as cuddly as you are."

Cuddly? Her? Ha. "I'm as cuddly as a porcupine."

His soft laugh told her he didn't believe her instinctive protestation. "You're very nice to hold, Manda. I can't decide which I like better—holding you in my arms while you sleep, or just watching you."

"You watch me sleep? Why?"

"You're soft when you're asleep," he explained simply.

Soft. He didn't mean her skin, or her hair. She knew what he meant, that he had seen her with her guard down, emotionally vulnerable, no barriers. And he sounded happy about it.

Her heart twisted a little. Then she kicked her legs restlessly. "Get back to the cotton candy," she ordered, preferring sexy talk to the gentle, tender stuff. It was safer. Less risky.

"God, you're so predictable."

Gasping, she snapped, "I am not!"

"Yeah, babe, you are. You wanted to reach for your sex toy and let me whisper you through an orgasm and I went and got sappy on you."

Okay. So she was predictable. She didn't reply at first,

nibbling her lip, finally asking, "Does that mean no phone sex?"

"Are you kidding? Hell yeah to the phone sex." His voice lowered, all amusement fading from it as he admitted, "I'm lying here with my rock-hard cock in my hand, just thinking about all the places in your body I want to fill with it."

"Oh, my," she whispered, a few of those places reacting instinctively. Her mouth went dry, her sex very wet. She moved her hand in a long, slow slide down her bare stomach until she reached her hip. "Tell me more."

He did, speaking in a hoarse whisper. "I want to take you in every way a man can take a woman."

She closed her eyes, the very word *take* making her quiver. Amanda was not one to give up control. But oh, how she had enjoyed it that Friday night in Daytona. Giving herself over to him, knowing he wouldn't hurt her and only wanted to give her pleasure had been one of the most exciting sexual experiences of her life.

"But first we'd have to get rid of all that cotton candy."

"You want to take a shower together?" she teased.

"Not right away. No, first I want to lie on my back and pull you up on top of me."

Her pulse pounded, her breath became shallow.

"I want you sitting on my chest, your legs open for me so I can lick all that sugar off the insides of your creamy thighs."

Amanda's legs clenched reflexively. She moved her hands to the curls between them, sliding her fingertip over her clit, hissing at how hard and sensitive it was. Every word he uttered was an invisible caress, the mental picture he created almost drugging in its sensual intensity.

"It'll be soft and fluffy at first. So sweet. But the closer I get to you, the more pure sugar I'll find. Because you'll be so hot and wet it will already have melted."

"Oh, Reese." She arched on the bed, stroking her clit harder, then sliding her finger between the lips of her sex. *Hot and wet* most definitely described what she felt.

"Do you know how much I love having my tongue on you…in you?" he asked. "How good you taste to me?"

She reached for the sex toy in the drawer beside the bed. Now, more than ever, she wished she had a big, thick rubber one rather than just the thin plastic vibrator. She wanted to be filled. *Taken.*

"Manda?"

"I'm here," she whispered as she flipped the switch and moved the device right where she most needed it. Then she clarified, "Actually, I'm not here…I'm almost *there.*" Hearing his deep breaths, she knew she wasn't alone. "Tell me what happens next. After you've licked away every bit of sweetness."

"You tell me," he countered.

"Easy. I'll slide down your body. Slowly. Tormenting you."

"No fair. I didn't torment you."

He was tormenting her now. Giving her fantasy when she wanted reality. But fantasy would have to do, at least for now.

"But I wouldn't be able to hold out," she conceded. "I'd be so desperate to have you inside me, the second I felt the tip of your cock against me, I'd slide down onto it, welcoming you in one deep thrust."

He groaned. Hearing that deep, primal sound of pleasure, recognizing it from all the times Reese had come inside her, Amanda pressed the vibrator a little harder. The waves of her climax rolled up. Higher. Faster. She couldn't speak anymore, couldn't listen, couldn't even think. She could only feel as the pleasure exploded in a hot rush, filling her body.

But it was short-lived. Very short. Not nearly the kind of satisfaction she got in Reese Campbell's arms.

Silent and spent, gasping on the bed with the phone still beside her ear, she had to admit it, if only to herself. She'd become addicted to him.

And she knew, without a doubt, she'd do just about anything to be with him again. For as long as she could have him.

Christmas

SOME YEARS, THE CELEBRATION of Hanukkah coincided with Christmas. Fortunately, however, this year was not one of them.

Which meant two real holiday getaways in December.

They'd spent the first one in a room in a New York City hotel. Reese had met Amanda there, not sure what she had up her sleeve for them. The venue had been far different from the place in Florida where they'd spent Thanksgiving weekend.

Not that he'd complained. Just wanting to be with her again, he really hadn't cared where they went. That desire had grown exponentially after their Cotton Candy

Day phone sex, and he probably would have agreed to meet her in the middle of a war zone if that was the only way he could get her.

So, yeah, anyplace would do, as long as it had a bed and was far away from the real world where nobody knew them. A place where Amanda could relax and forget she wasn't the settling-down type, that she didn't want a relationship, was just fine with him.

Especially since, whether she liked it or not—whether she would admit it or not—they *had* a relationship.

Far from a beachfront dive, the Manhattan high-rise had been all about luxury and indulgence. He'd understood her reason for choosing it when she'd finally revealed herself…and the game. Reese had nearly had a heart attack when she'd snuck out of the closet in their room, dressed all in black from head to toe. She was playing the part of a cat burglar who'd just been caught in the act.

He'd really liked the way she'd taken possession of his most valuable jewels.

He'd liked it just as much that she hadn't resisted when he'd whisked her out of the hotel for dinner at an upscale restaurant. And that she'd given him a loud, smacking kiss when he'd presented her not with tickets to a Broadway show but with ones to a hard-rock concert at the Garden.

During the trip, she'd been relaxed—sexy as always, but not so guarded. She'd laughed easily, talked more. It was as if she'd done some thinking after their walk on the beach, and had decided to just go with this for as long as it lasted.

His Easter eggs were looking brighter already.

The thought of it made him smile. Especially since he was going to be seeing her again so soon.

"I still can't believe you're taking off for Las Vegas on Christmas. That's so mean!"

Ignoring the disgruntled tone of his teenage sister, Molly, he forced his thoughts off tomorrow's trip—technically, the day *after* Christmas—and turned them back to the matter at hand: the board game which was set up on the kitchen table. Playing games after Christmas dinner had been a Campbell family tradition since he was a kid.

That his father had been the game fanatic made the ritual one everyone seemed to want to keep alive. Including Reese, even though, on any other day of the year, he'd rather eat moldy fruitcake than play Risk.

Then again, it could be worse. There had been those Pretty, Pretty Princess marathons all those years ago when his sisters were young and got their way most of the time.

Hmm. Not that much had changed. Even though he wasn't the pushover his dad had been when it came to the Campbell girls, they still managed to get what they wanted for the most part.

Like now.

"Wahoo! I just took over Australia! You keep thinking about the chick you're hooking up with in Vegas, big brother, and I'll keep taking your countries."

Reese frowned at his sister Debra, nine years his junior and halfway through her second year of college. She smirked, lifting a challenging brow, daring him to deny what she'd said.

"What?" Molly asked, her eyes widening. "You're meeting someone? Who?" The sixteen-year-old, who hadn't yet figured out that the world didn't revolve entirely around her, pouted as she added, "Is that why you won't take us, even though you *know* how much I'm dying to go to Vegas? Because you want to hook up with some girl? Talk about shitty."

"Watch your mouth," he said, the reply automatic. Funny, considering when he was sixteen, his bad language had prompted their mother to squirt a bottle of dish detergent all over his dinner one night. But he figured it's what Dad would have said.

"Why would *you* want to go, anyway? All you'd do is shop for clothes and text with your friends, just like you do here."

That was the longest sentence Reese had heard out of his kid brother Jack's mouth all day. The fourteen-year-old had eased up on his I-hate-everyone-because-I'm-a-teenager schtick a little bit today, and for him, the remark was downright chatty. He even went on to add, "Who's the girl, Reese?"

As pleased as he was that his sullen brother, who'd been only twelve when their father had died, was actually interested in having a conversation, that was one talk he didn't want to have. "Ignore her. She's trying to distract you so she can take over Southeast Asia."

"Is she hot?"

Incendiary. "Are we playing or are we talking?" He glanced at his watch. "Because it's almost eight and I'm outta here at nine whether I control the entire world or not."

Jack wasn't put off. Neither were his sisters. Like three dogs sniffing after a bone, they stayed on the subject. He was just lucky his other two sisters—Tess, a hard-assed, divorced man-hater right now, and Bonnie, the bleeding heart who wanted to save the world—were in the other room watching Tess's kids play with their new toys.

"Is your new girlfriend the reason you went away for Thanksgiving weekend?" asked Molly, that whine in her voice making his eye twitch.

"Friend," he clarified.

Molly rolled her eyes. "Does she live far away?"

"Chicago," Debra said.

Reese gaped. "How the hell do you know that?"

"Aunt Jean told me," she said with a broad, self-satisfied grin. Debra had outgrown any teenage whininess and now just loved playing her role of family shit-stirrer.

Reese didn't ask how Aunt Jean knew. The old woman had spies watching her spies. Besides, if he wanted to know, he could ask her himself. She should be here soon; they would be the last stop on her around-Pennsylvania visits to all her nieces, nephews and distant family members.

But he didn't want to know. In fact, he didn't want to see her at all, knowing she'd take one look at him and crow with triumph. Obviously, if she was telling his kid sister about his trips to meet Amanda, she knew damn well he'd taken her advice—well, her order—to go out and live a little.

Nobody said "I told you so" like an old woman who really *had* told you so. With any luck, he'd be gone before she got here to say it.

"Why hasn't this 'friend' come to meet us?" asked Molly.

"Maybe because you'd scare her into the next state."

"Oh, a real Miss Priss, huh?" the sixteen-year-old said with a tsk. "No balls?"

Jack grunted. "I sure hope not. If Reese switches sides and starts tea-bagging, I'm giving up on this family for good."

His jaw hanging open, he stared at his kid brother. "If I start *what?*"

"You know, it's when you…"

Reese threw a hand up, palm out. "Enough. I know what it is." Glancing at his sisters, who made faces ranging from ewwwy to grossed-out, he saw they knew what it was, too.

Jesus, how had his father ever stood it? Teenagers were a damned nightmare.

"What's her name?" Molly asked.

"None of your business."

"None of Your Business Campbell. Has a nice ring to it," said Debra, her pretty eyes dancing with laughter. She was the mischief-maker of the bunch, playing that middle-child role like she'd invented it. "You can name your kids Go Away and Bite Me."

"Go away," he mumbled, closing his eyes and rubbing at them with his fingers.

"Bite me," she said sweetly.

"That's not very polite, young lady."

His eyes flying open, he looked up to see his great-aunt Jean standing in the doorway. Surveying the scene, she looked matriarchal, though her lips twitched with amusement. He suspected she'd been there for a while.

His sisters both rose from the table to greet their aunt who, though an eccentric one, was also everybody's favorite. He suspected that was partly due to the fact that she always came loaded for bear with presents.

"Help me unload my car, will you? I brought a few goodies."

The girls raced toward the door so fast the Risk board almost went flying. Which would have been fine with him.

"Gonna help them, bro?" Reese asked Jack, who had slouched down in his seat, not wanting to appear eager or excited about anything. Around the immediate family, he'd lowered his defenses for a little while today. Aunt Jean's arrival had put that guarded look back in his eyes.

Reese's heart twisted. The kid had once been a happy-go-lucky, smiling Little Leaguer. But not anymore. Fourteen was bad enough. With the weight Jack had been carrying around for two years, it was a lot worse.

The boy shrugged. "Whatever."

As his brother got up and walked by, Reese couldn't help offering a small, encouraging nod, and a slight squeeze of his bony shoulder. *Be a kid. Just for tonight, even. Tomorrow's soon enough to go back to being mad at the world.*

Jack didn't smile in return. But his spine might have straightened a little and his trudging footsteps picked up. It was something, anyway.

"He'll be all right," Aunt Jean murmured, her eyes softer than usual as they watched Jack walk out the back door.

Reese sincerely hoped so.

"Now, let's talk about *you*."

He had known that was coming. "I hear you already have been. Thanks a lot. I really love getting the third degree from my sisters."

"And a merry Christmas to you, too."

Curiosity won out over embarrassment. "So how'd you know?"

She merely shrugged, guarding that mysterious, all-knowing, all-seeing reputation. Then, glancing at her diamond watch, she shook her head. "Hadn't you better be heading home for the night? It's a long trip to Las Vegas." She shrugged. "I'm afraid I don't have very much for you in the car, because I think I've already given you a big enough gift this year."

Well, he supposed her urging him to go out and have an adventure for himself did count as a gift. Because, whether he wanted to admit it or not, the past few months had been the best he'd had in a long, *long* time.

Reese's mouth widened in a smile and he crossed the room to kiss her powdery, paper-thin cheek. "Thank you, Aunt Jean."

"You're welcome. Now, go. Have fun. Be wild." She waved a hand, gesturing around the kitchen. "This domestic bliss will all be here waiting for you when you get back."

Whether that was a promise, or a threat, he didn't know. Nor did he really want to think about it. Because he already had other things on his mind.

He had the rest of a holiday to celebrate. And a woman he was crazy about to share it with.

AMANDA WASN'T MUCH of a Christmas person. Her parents had not believed in spoiling her or her sister, so the season had never really entailed presents or parties. The holidays comprised a lot of volunteer work, the requisite Bing Crosby songs, quiet dinners and church. Some years, they hadn't even gotten a tree, her frugal father finding the expense excessive.

The Christmases she'd spent with Uncle Frank had been completely different. Big parties, lots of drinking, dancing, jetting off to some hot spot for New Year's. There had definitely been no popcorn stringing or chestnuts roasting.

The closest she ever came to a normal American family holiday were the years she'd stayed in Chicago and had gone to Jazz's parents' house. But she'd always felt a bit like an outsider. She didn't quite get the lingo, had never felt completely comfortable receiving socks and bras from Jazz's mom, who treated her just like one of her own.

Christmas, she had long ago decided, just wasn't her thing.

So when Reese Campbell walked into their hotel room with a suitcase full of presents for her, she didn't know what to think. "Oh, God, are you kidding? I only got you one small gift!"

A small, sexy gift. A small, sexy, *funny* gift.

But she didn't think the men's velvet boxers with the Rudolph head—complete with blinking red nose—was quite equal to the ten or so packages he pulled out and tossed onto the big bed.

"I'm so bad at this," she groaned, not elaborating. He knew what she meant: this whole *girlfriend* thing. No, they weren't using the word, but it was about the only one she could come up with. And as girlfriends went, she totally sucked the big one.

Metaphorically speaking. Well, literally speaking, too, but thinking about that wasn't going to help right at this particular moment.

"I don't care. Christmas isn't about getting, it's about giving."

"You're giving me a guilty conscience," she wailed, staring at the brightly wrapped boxes.

Funny, a few months ago, her first instinct would probably have been to give in to the tightness squeezing her chest, turn and walk out the door. She'd always wanted to visit London during the winter. Prague sounded good. Amsterdam.

No. You're not doing that. Not this time. Not to him.

She'd come here this weekend knowing full well what it meant. After their conversation in Florida, she knew the terms had changed yet again. Their New York trip had been fun, but Christmas and a whole week in Vegas together added up to something more. And while she'd managed to convince herself nothing would be really different, that this was just another sexy holiday getaway, deep down she'd known Reese might treat it as a genuine one between two people who were involved.

And she'd shown up with damned fuzzy Rudolph boxer shorts.

Tart, sour and heartless. That was her.

"Don't even think about it," he warned, obviously seeing something in her eye.

She didn't need his warning. Because even without it, she'd already kept her feet planted on the floor.

The pressure in her chest gradually eased until she could breathe normally again. Then, instead of frowning and accusing him of taking things too seriously, getting her gifts like they were some kind of real couple, she couldn't help but smile.

"You're serious? All these are for me?"

"Well," he admitted as he threw himself down on the bed, "some of them are for me, too." He wagged his brows suggestively as he rolled onto his side, resting on his bent elbow. "I think a fashion show is in order."

She bit the inside of her cheek to keep from laughing. "Okay, but only if you promise to do one, too, with what I got you."

"You're on."

Oh, boy, was he going to regret that one. But Amanda could hardly wait.

Well, giving it some thought, she realized she could wait. There was a way to salvage this situation. "Listen, let's hold off on the presents until tomorrow, okay? Give me a little time to at least come up with an ugly tie, a bowling ball or a bottle of Hai Karate for you to open."

He snorted a laugh. "You just described every one of my father's Christmas mornings. But, bad news. I don't bowl."

"Okay. Maybe I can come up with something else."

He sat up, reaching for her hand and tugging her forward until she stood between his legs. "You really don't have to."

"I know." She wanted to. Suddenly, the idea of giving her lover a real Christmas gift sounded like exactly the right thing to do.

There was something else she wanted to do, as well. Something that had been on her mind for days, ever since she'd realized they were going to sin city. She had a fantasy in mind, one she suspected he was going to enjoy sharing.

"You do realize today is a holiday, too. It's Boxing Day."

"I'm not into boxing, either," he said, his eyes twinkling.

"It's a big deal in some countries." She shimmied out from between his strong legs. "What I'm trying to say is, I would very much like to *play* with you on this holiday."

He nodded slowly, the twinkle turning into a gleam of interest. Hunger.

"So here's what I want you to do." She dug a piece of paper out of her pants pocket and shoved it toward him. "Go to this address and wait for me. I'll be there in an hour."

He glanced at it. "Is it a restaurant or something?"

She shook her head. "No. Just wait outside."

Still appearing puzzled, he rose to his feet. But he didn't leave immediately, pausing to cup her chin and tug her toward him for a soft, slow kiss goodbye.

She almost relented, giving up on the fantasy for some good, old-fashioned, lovely sex. But she'd been thinking about this for a long time. After showing up without any presents for him, the least she could do was try to give him the kind of fantasy he would never forget.

And just about every man in the world had one fantasy when it came to Vegas. Reese's was going to come true.

Pushing him toward the door, she said, "Go. One hour."

He lifted his hand in mock salute. "I can hardly wait."

The minute he was gone, Amanda raced to her suitcase and began yanking clothes from it. She'd done a little more eBay shopping, looking for another costume. Not a stewardess this time, she was going for someone quite different.

She intended to transform herself completely. And

fifteen minutes later, when she looked at her reflection in the mirror, she knew she had succeeded.

"Hot damn," she whispered, smiling as she checked herself out from bottom to top.

The boots were even more kick-ass than her Halloween ones. Black leather, spiked, coming all the way up over her knee. They were wicked and screamed sex.

Above them was a large expanse of fishnet-covered thighs. And finally a few inches of hot pink miniskirt that barely covered her ass. It was made out of something that felt like cellophane and crinkled when she walked.

The teensy, tie-front white top covered her shoulders and her breasts and not much else. And the short, platinum-blond wig completed her transformation from Amanda Bauer, professional pilot, to Mandy the hooker.

After all, what guy hadn't fantasized about being picked up by a sexy call girl in Vegas?

"Whatever the customer wants, that's what he's going to get," she whispered, smiling as she headed for the door to the room. She paused only to grab her long coat off the back of a chair. Not only because it was chilly out, but also because there was no way she wanted any hotel employees to see her entire costume. The place was five star all the way, and the *Pretty Woman* look probably wouldn't be welcome in the lobby.

"Okay, sweet man, get ready, because here I come," she said under her breath as she descended in the elevator. Every minute ensured her certainty of one thing.

Reese Campbell had no idea what kind of night he was in for.

7

Boxing Day

SHOWGIRL OR STRIPPER? Paid escort? Call girl?

Reese wasn't sure which Amanda was going to show up tonight. He only knew that whichever woman met him here on this slightly seedy corner, one block off the northernmost end of the Strip, she was going to blow his mind. Just like she always did.

"Come on, it's been over an hour," he muttered, glancing at his watch as he leaned against a light post. She'd better show up soon, or one of the real working girls might decide he was looking for some company.

She'd been adorable when pushing him out of the room back at the hotel. Had she really thought he didn't know, that he couldn't figure out what kinds of games she'd want to play in Las Vegas? Seriously, what could be more obvious?

Still, maybe it wasn't as clear to her as it was to him that he knew her so well. Better than he'd ever imagined when they first met. Better than she'd ever wanted him to, that was for sure.

He was even beginning to understand why. Despite

those careful walls she'd kept around herself in the beginning, during their last couple of get-togethers, she had started to reveal bits and pieces of herself.

She'd talked a little about her family back home, hinting at a lack of connection that saddened him on her behalf. His own family might drive him crazy, but he'd been raised in a house filled to the brim with love.

He suspected Amanda had never been assured of that emotion from her parents.

She'd also asked about his upbringing, and in her slightly wistful tone, he'd heard much more than she was willing to say out loud. He'd known, somehow, that despite how much she claimed not to need anyone, a part of her might actually wonder what such connections might be like.

One thing she hadn't talked any more about was her past love life. But, hell, she didn't need to. He knew she'd had a few rocky relationships. He also knew they'd ended badly, and that she still kicked herself about it.

She was human, wasn't she? Human and only in her late twenties. Who the hell didn't do dumb things in their twenties, things they regretted for a long time after? Amanda simply hadn't realized yet that she wasn't much different from anybody else. Including him.

"Hey stranger, you lookin' for some company?"

Call girl.

Excitement washed over him as he turned to stare at the woman who'd spoken from a few feet away. She stood just outside a puddle of illumination cast by the streetlight, and he couldn't see her well. But he'd know her anywhere. That voice, that scent. The very air seemed filled with static electricity, snapping with the excitement that always surrounded her. He reacted to it on a visceral level, as he had since the moment they'd met.

"Maybe," he admitted. "Are you offering to keep me company?"

"I might be willing to do that. If you offer me enough...incentive."

She sauntered closer, into the light, and Reese had to suck in a surprised breath. Good thing he'd had that moment of instant recognition, all his other senses confirming her identity. Because for a brief second, when he saw her, he feared he'd been mistaken. At first glance, she looked like a completely different woman. An incredibly sexy woman. A woman he wanted with every cell in his body.

"Wow," he muttered.

Her wig was short, blond, curling just past her chin. The style emphasized the heavy makeup she wore. Amanda's face was already lovely, but with the added coloring—the thick mascara, the ruby-red lips—she looked exotic and oozed sex appeal.

The clothes, however, took the sex appeal from oozing to gushing.

Her long, black overcoat clung to the very edges of her shoulders. Completely unbuttoned, it gaped open to reveal the skimpy outfit beneath. What little of it there was.

Her white top was not only incredibly tiny, plunging low to tie beneath her breasts, it was also thin, nearly sheer. Even in the low light, he could make out the dark, puckered nipples and hunger flooded his mouth. It had been too long since he'd tasted her, touched her. He should have insisted on at least a few minutes back at the hotel to satisfy the raging need he'd been feeling ever since they'd parted ways in New York.

Her midriff was entirely bare, down all the way past her stomach. The skirt, which didn't even reach her belly button, merely pretended to clothe her hips, and was so tight he could see the line where her thighs came together underneath. And oh, those fishnet-clad thighs beckoned him, tempting him to taste the tiny squares of supple skin revealed between the black, stretchy bits of fabric.

The boots were, without a doubt, his favorite part of the whole thing. And he already knew he was going to rip those hose off her body so she could leave the boots on to wrap around him as he pounded into her.

"So, whaddya say, mister?"

"To what?"

"To a date?"

"A…date? With you?" he asked, pretending reticence he in no way felt.

"No," she said with a definite eye roll. "With that light post holding you up."

He still didn't move.

"Come on, admit it. Haven't you fantasized about spending a night with a girl like me?"

He couldn't answer that. Not truthfully. Because if he answered in the game, as if she were really a call girl, he'd have to say no. He'd never even thought about being with a prostitute.

If he answered as himself, the real Reese Campbell talking to the real Amanda Bauer, then the response was unequivocally yes. He wanted to go out with *her,* be a half of a couple with her—Amanda—almost as much as he wanted to take her back to the hotel and do her until she screamed with pleasure.

"I promise you, I'll let you do things to me that your nice little wife or girlfriend back home has never even heard of."

Interesting. The corner of his mouth lifted in a half smile. "I think I might need to hear more about these things before I make a decision."

She moved closer, her gait slinky, the sway of her hips exaggerated. When she reached his side, she lifted her hand to his chest. "Let's just say you can do anything you want to me. Absolutely *anything*. And I'd let you."

He shook his head, feigning confusion. "I'm still not sure I know what you mean."

She lifted her chin and her eyes narrowed as she heard the challenge in his voice. Then, with a smile of pure wickedness, she leaned up on her toes, coming close enough for her beautiful lips to graze his cheek. With a nip on his earlobe, she told him one *very* naughty thing she wanted him to do to her.

Damn. Heat and excitement flared and he slid his hands into her coat, cupping her waist. Without a word, he turned her around, so her back was to the light pole, then bent down and kissed her. Licking his way into her mouth, he met her tongue with his and thrust lazily. Their bodies melded and he heard her tiny groan when she felt how hard he already was for her. She pressed against him, grinding her groin against his erection, wrapping one long leg around his to cup him more intimately between her thighs.

They were on a public street and it was only ten o'clock at night. Fortunately, though, the cool weather had people staying inside the closest casino gambling, not outside cruising the block. So as far as he could tell, they didn't have an audience.

That was good. Because he couldn't stop. No *way* would he stop. Not when her lips were so sweet and her body so willing. Not when she'd whispered such wanton, erotic desires in his ear, promising their fulfillment with her dreamy-eyed stare.

When he finally ended the kiss, lifted his head and looked down at her, he saw the dazed look of pure want on her face. Her lids half covered her green eyes and most of her lipstick had been kissed off. She looked sensual and awakened, ready for sin and sex and more of everything they'd ever done together. And some things they hadn't.

He had to have her. *Had* to.

"Let's get out of here," he muttered, already stepping toward the curb to flag down a taxi.

"Absolutely," she whispered, her voice shaking.

Traffic wasn't heavy, and not a cab was in sight. Figured. When he saw one crossing the next block, Reese stepped off the curb onto the street, whistling loudly. But before he could see whether the cabbie had heard him and made a last-minute turn, he was startled by a shout that split the night air.

"Stop, thief!"

Reese froze, jerking his head to stare in the direction of the voice. The cry had sounded like it was coming from the closest building, which had a sign identifying it as a pawn shop.

He was a split second slow in reacting. If he'd been thinking more clearly, he would have immediately jumped back up onto the sidewalk, grabbed Amanda and shoved her safely behind him. In his surprise, though, he hadn't done it.

So she was right in the path of the black-cloaked figure that came hurtling out from behind the building.

"Manda!" he cried, seeing the shape emerge from the darkness.

Before she had time to react, the running man barreled into her. They stumbled around together for a second, their legs and coats tangling.

"You son of a bitch." Reese dove toward them, knocking the man off her, but falling, himself, in the process. "You're dead," he snarled.

The thief, obviously realizing there was only one thing that would stop Reese from chasing him down and beating him to a pulp, whirled around toward Amanda and shoved. Hard.

The blow sent her careening toward the street. Those high-heeled boots wobbled, making it impossible for her to catch her balance. Right before she fell off the curb into the path of the cab, which had indeed turned and was rapidly cruising up the block, Reese lunged to his feet and grabbed her around the waist, hauling her back to safety.

"My God, are you okay?"

She nodded, though her whole body was shaking, especially as a taxi screeched to a stop right where she would have landed in the street.

"That rotten bastard," Reese snapped, his feet nearly in motion to go after the man in black. The thief had just darted down the next alleyway, heading across a debris-laden, abandoned construction site that separated this road from the north strip.

"No, Reese," she insisted, holding on to his arm. "I'm

fine, really. And you are *not* going to go chasing after some robber. You could get hurt."

"He was a scrawny runt."

"Who might be armed. You're staying right here."

Before he could reply, a heavyset, balding man with flaming red cheeks jogged up to them. "Did you see him? Did you get a good look? Rotten thief robbed my shop!"

"I saw him," Amanda replied, sounding weary.

The shop owner peered at her, narrowed his eyes and sighed heavily. "Oh, that's just *great*."

The man's sneer toward Amanda, whom he obviously took for a real lady of the evening, tempted Reese to let the guy deal with his own problems. But his rage toward the thug who'd so callously tossed her into the street was greater. So he admitted, "I saw him, too. Now why don't you go call the police so we can give them a description." He tightened his arm around Amanda's shoulders. "And hurry. We've got things to do tonight."

OF ALL THE WAYS she'd envisioned spending their first night in Vegas, standing in a dingy pawn shop, talking to two officers from the LVPD, hadn't been in the top thousand. Especially because said cops had spent the first ten minutes of their interview trying to figure out whether they needed to arrest her for prostitution and Reese for solicitation.

Talk about a convincing costume. She and Reese had finally had to come clean about what they were up to, showing their credentials, including Amanda's pilot's license. Ever since, the younger police officer had been trying to hide a smile and was casting quick, sneaky glances at Amanda whenever he thought he could get away with it. The older one hadn't even tried to hide his amusement. She'd swear she heard him mumbling something about how much he wished his wife would wear thigh-high boots.

That so didn't help.

"Okay then, miss, sir, I think I've got everything I need," said the older officer, who'd introduced himself as Parker. Standing in the well-lit entranceway of the shop, they'd just finished answering all his questions. "You did a good job remembering details about this guy."

Amanda didn't think she would soon forget the pale, pockmarked face of the man who'd so readily shoved her toward what could have been her death. His glazed brown eyes and long, greasy blond hair weren't going to leave her mind anytime soon, either.

"The owner of the shop says the thief got away with some valuable diamond jewelry," Parker added. He snapped his notebook closed and tucked it into his uniform pocket.

Reese glanced around the small, nondescript shop, which was a little dusty and unimpressive. "Really?" he asked, sounding doubtful. "It doesn't look exactly top shelf."

"You'd be surprised," offered the younger officer, whom the older one kept calling Rookie. His voice low, he looked around for the owner, who'd disappeared into the back to do yet another check on his inventory. "A lotta these places are mob-owned, legit businesses where money goes to get nice and clean."

"Would you shut yer yap?" said Parker. With a glare, he explained, "We're really not in the habit of making unfounded comments about members of our local business community."

The younger guy snapped his mouth shut and didn't say another word.

"If we're finished, are we free to go?" Reese asked.

"Sure thing." Smiling, Parker tipped his hat at Amanda. "Hope you two enjoy the rest of your visit to our fair city. And might I suggest that next time you, uh, confine your field trips to the lobby of your own hotel?"

Though she'd been embarrassed at first, now all Amanda could do was chuckle. Parker seemed like a nice guy, and, really, it was either laugh or cry. Laughing seemed the much better option.

"You bet," she said. Winking, she added, "And if you get your wife a pair of these boots, be sure to get one size larger than she usually wears. They're pretty painful."

He threw his head back and guffawed. "If I came home with a pair of those things for her, she'd use them to kick my ass."

With a polite nod, Reese led Amanda out of the shop by the arm. She was still chuckling as they emerged outside, knowing she was going to have to share this whole story with Jazz. Her friend would love it.

So would Uncle Frank, if she was ever able to get over the whole embarrassment factor and tell him, too. But it was the kind of situation that would horrify her parents, and reinforce their firm belief that she was a reckless wanton who cared nothing for her own reputation. Or theirs.

Caught up in thought, she didn't notice that a small crowd had gathered outside the pawn shop. About a dozen people milled around on the sidewalk, likely drawn by the flash of the police lights and the whispers of a robbery in the neighborhood.

"Hey, what happened?" somebody asked.

"You'll have to let the police fill you in," Reese said, sliding a hand around her waist as he tried to lead her through the crowd.

It was only when she felt the warmth of his fingers against her very bare skin that she realized she hadn't re-buttoned her coat, which she'd unfastened in the heat of the store. Gaping open, it revealed her costume in all its glory to the wide-eyed strangers. She reached for the edges of it, intending to yank it closed. But before she could, a male voice called, "Hey, sweet thing, how late you working tonight?"

Another one added, "Got a business card?"

Though she knew she should be absolutely mortified, and maybe even a little nervous, more laughter bubbled up inside her. The size of the crowd, the presence of a few normally dressed women and tourists, and the two police officers right inside the closest building eased her hint of fear.

And the embarrassment? Hell, she was so far past that, she couldn't even remember what it felt like.

Beside her, Reese made a small sound. Worried, she glanced over and saw his lips twitch. Relief flowed through her. His anger and concern had finally eased up and he was beginning to see the humor in the situation, too.

"Sorry, guys, she's retired," he said, tugging her closer to his side.

"Since when?"

Following his lead, she sidled closer to Reese. Glued to his side from ankle to hip, she slipped her arm around his waist, too. Dropping her head onto his shoulder and simpering a little, she pointed toward a small white building across the street. "Since I roped myself a man tonight at that wedding chapel over there. Jeez, what's a girl gotta do to enjoy her wedding night?"

The two potential clients groaned, but the others surrounding them started to laugh and call out congratulations. They were probably going to go back home and tell their friends and family they'd stumbled into a real-life version of *Pretty Woman.*

Reese, wicked amusement dancing in his eyes, took full advantage, playing to the crowd. Without warning, he tugged her closer, turning her so their faces were inches apart, then he caught her mouth in a deep, intimate kiss.

She forgot about everything for a full minute. The robbery, the thug, the cops, the onlookers. When Reese kissed her like this, all hot and wet, with delicious strokes of his tongue, everything else just ceased to exist.

When they finally ended the kiss, it was to the sound of applause. "Way to go, girlfriend!" someone yelled.

She didn't have to force the note of breathless excitement as she asked, "Can we please get outta here, hubby-cakes?"

"You got it, sugar-britches," Reese replied, compressing his lips, trying so hard not to laugh.

He amazed her. From sexy playmate, to hero who'd literally saved her butt, to serious witness, to passionate lover, and back to the most playful, good-humored, self-confident man she'd ever known, all in the span of an hour.

She'd known before tonight that Reese Campbell was a great guy. But as she let him lead her away, holding her protectively, lovingly, like a new husband with his bride, she had to acknowledge that he was even more than that.

He was special. Very special. The kind of man women read about in romance novels and dreamed about actually meeting.

He was, to use his favorite word, just about perfect.

Perfect for her? Well, that she wasn't ready to concede, at least not in the long term. But for right now, there was simply no place else she'd rather be...and no one else on earth she'd rather be with.

New Year's Eve

THEY SPENT THE ENTIRE holiday week in Las Vegas. And this time, after that first night when their game playing had nearly gotten them into legal trouble, they'd let all the other identities fade away. It was just Reese and Amanda, spending every minute of the day together.

They gambled, they saw a few shows, they walked the strip and shopped. They laughed over pizza dinners and shared a bucket of popcorn as they went to see a movie, which neither of them had done for so long.

And finally, eventually, they even talked.

"You're sure you don't mind leaving before midnight?" Amanda asked as they reentered their room at around eleven-thirty on New Year's Eve.

"My ears have been ringing all week from the sound of the slot machines. Add a few thousand voices screaming 'Happy New Year' and I might go deaf." Before he'd even reached back to lock the door, he drew her into his arms and kissed her cheek. "In other words, no, I most definitely do not mind sharing a quiet celebration with you."

Though he had never seen her drink much, Amanda had enjoyed a couple of glasses of champagne at the hotel's holiday party downstairs. Though not drunk, he'd have to describe her as slightly tipsy. Her eyes sparkled and her always beautiful smile flashed a little wider. Though nobody would ever call her giddy, when she kicked off her shoes and spun around the room with her arms extended straight out, she looked pretty darn close.

She also looked damn near adorable—young and carefree. Her black cocktail dress was tight to the waist, but flared on the bottom and it swirled prettily around her bare legs.

"I love New Year's," she admitted once she stopped twirling.

He never had understood the appeal of the holiday himself, having grown up hearing his father calling it amateur night: the night normally smart, rational people drank too much then drove drunk. In their line of work, they knew way too much about it. The Campbells had always stayed home on New Year's Eve.

"It doesn't sound like the kind of holiday your family would be into," he said, his tone careful, as always, when the subject of her family life came up.

Amanda laughed out loud. "Are you kidding? Hell no, they weren't into it." Her voice lowered and her brow pulled down in a deep frown. "'This holiday is just an excuse for people to use poor judgment and do things they know are immoral and indecent. No daughter of mine is going to participate in public drunkenness or lewdity.'"

The imitation had to be of her father, though, honestly, he couldn't imagine this woman having grown up with someone like that. "Not exactly Mr. Tender Loving Care?"

She snorted. "I don't think he knows the meaning of any of those words." She thought about it, then clarified. "Well, *mister* he gets very well. He has kept my mother in her place since the minute he proposed to her. But *tender, loving* and *care* just aren't part of his vocabulary. Not toward her, not toward *anyone*." She yawned widely, as if she were discussing something mundane rather than utterly heartbreaking. "And I guess living with him all these years has rubbed off. Because my mother is about as warm as a guppy, too."

He glanced away so she wouldn't see the sudden flash of sympathy—and even anger—in his face. There was no malice in her. This wasn't an adult kid blaming her poor, unknowing parents for some imaginary slights. She didn't even sound resentful. She'd simply accepted their frigidity as a fact and moved on.

How much of their coldness had she unintentionally absorbed? How deeply had it affected her own life, her choices, the face she showed to the world? Seeing her like this, hearing the truths she'd been trying to hide from him since the very beginning, he understood so much more...and he liked her all the more for it. Even though he knew she would probably resent any sympathy he tried to offer.

He forced the thoughts away, as well as the unpleasant subject of what her parents had or hadn't given her in her childhood. Not wanting her to even think about it anymore, he changed the subject. "So when did you become a New Year's convert?"

She plopped down onto the edge of the bed. "In college. My freshman boyfriend took me to my very first

New Year's Eve party and I got completely caught up in everyone else's excitement and good mood."

He hid his interest in the "boyfriend" part.

"I loved all the resolutions, the anticipation of a clean slate, a fresh start. And I suddenly saw it as a chance to reevaluate, figure out what went wrong in the past year and plan on how to make it right in the coming one."

Interesting. He had to wonder what she had evaluated and planned on this particular holiday. But he knew better than to ask. He shrugged out of his suit jacket and tossed it aside, then sat in a chair opposite the bed, eyeing her. "What did you decide that first year?"

"To dump my boyfriend."

Caught off guard, he had to chuckle. While that subject had been taboo up until now, Amanda laughed, as well. "He was a creeper," she admitted.

"A…creeper?"

"He had moist hands and he was sneaky, always touching me. That was when I was only nineteen, and still a virgin."

She'd held on to her virginity longer than most girls he knew. Considering her family background, he wasn't entirely surprised. He doubted there had been much dating or teenage partying in her household.

"So we have the creeper," he murmured, lifting his index finger to count off. "Who was next?"

Probably because she'd had a couple of drinks, Amanda didn't immediately freeze him out and change the subject. Instead, she threw herself back on the bed, her brow scrunched as she thought about it.

"I dated around when I was a sophomore. Kind of a lot." The way she nibbled her lip told him what that meant. She'd lost that pesky virginity and had gone for a walk on the wild side.

"Then I hooked up with a guy named Scott for several months. I broke up with him when I caught him copying the answers from my take-home exam for a class we had together. After that came Tommy…he drove a Porsche and I think I liked the car more than I liked him, which he eventually figured out."

"Completely understandable," he pointed out.

She ignored him. "Rick was nice, but the first time we slept together and I realized he was lousy in the sack, I stopped taking his calls."

Again, completely understandable, at least for a college-aged kid. Not that he intended to interrupt her again, not now, when she seemed to really be getting to the nitty-gritty.

She was now the one with her fingers up. Mumbling under her breath, she lifted another, then another, and then moved on to her next hand. Up came the index finger. The middle one, then a third…which she quickly put back down. "Wait, Josh doesn't really count."

"Why not?" he asked, amused by this frank, open Amanda talking about her past. Even if she was only being that way because she'd had one too many sips of champagne.

"Because I was just a beard. I found out he was in the closet on our second date, but kept going out with him just 'cause he was a nice guy. Plus he had a crush on my roommate's boyfriend, who I hated, and it made me laugh to keep him around." Sitting up quickly, she gave him a stricken look. "Oh, that was bitchy, wasn't it? I *told* you."

"Yeah, yeah, you're cast-iron, babe."

So far, from what he could tell, she'd had about the same number of boyfriends as his twenty-something-year-old sisters. The difference being, from what he had pieced together in the past, that she had always been the one to walk away.

That refrain repeated in his mind. *She always walked away.*

He should have taken that as a warning sign, proceeded with caution. But he hadn't…mostly because he wasn't at all convinced Amanda was as anti-love-and-commitment as she claimed. She'd just never been involved with the right man. Whether that was pure happenstance, or by design—since her upbringing had to have soured her on the whole idea of personal relationships—he didn't know.

"Come to think of it, I don't feel so bad," she suddenly said with a firm nod. "I didn't break his heart or anything, so he had no business joining that Facebook group." Her voice lowered. "No business at all."

"What group?"

She hesitated, the finally admitted, "The 'Dumped by Amanda Bauer' group."

He threw back his head and laughed…until he saw that she wasn't smiling. Instead, her eyes held a hint of moisture and her bottom lip quivered. The tough girl actually looked vulnerable. Hurt.

Mentally kicking himself, he got up and joined her on the bed, pulling her into his arms. She burrowed into his chest, sniffing a tiny bit, and he suddenly had the urge to hunt down the pricks who'd formed the mean little club and made her cry.

Talk about ridiculous—holding on to some bullshit college gripes and sharing them with the world years later, no matter who you wounded. It was one way in which the Internet age definitely had not improved life.

Amanda let herself relax against him for a minute or two, then she began to tense, shifting uncomfortably. He recognized the signs and knew what she was thinking: too much emotion, too much talking, too personal, too dangerous.

He released her, forcing a smile. "It's almost midnight."

She didn't smile back, her beautiful face still wearing that same sad, stricken expression. Amanda stared at him for a long moment, her green eyes revealing her every thought as her gaze traveled over his face, as if to memorize him for the not-too-distant future when she wouldn't see him anymore.

"He wasn't the last one," she admitted.

"You don't have to do this...."

She ignored him. "The last guy I dated decided if I wouldn't just *give* him my undivided attention and devotion, he'd take it from me."

He didn't like the sound of this, not one bit.

"We had a fight, I broke it off, then he called in the middle of one night saying he'd just swallowed a bottle of pills."

Oh, God. Whether she wanted it or not, he had to hold her, tightly, giving her the support and tenderness she never asked for. He kissed her hair, whispering, "It wasn't your fault...."

She immediately shook her head. "No, he didn't die or anything."

Thank God.

"Because he was lying. The whole thing had been a setup, just to play on my emotions."

"What's his name?" he snarled, ready to kill a guy he'd just been thankful hadn't died.

"It doesn't matter. It's all over, all in the past. The point is…" She hesitated, then, with a voice as shaky as her slowly indrawn breath, whispered, "Don't love me, Reese."

His heart broke a little. For the pain of her past affairs, for the heartbreaks, and for the cold family life she'd endured. They'd combined to create a beautiful, extremely lovable woman who didn't think she was capable of returning the emotion.

She was wrong. She wouldn't admit it, not now, maybe not for a long time. But he knew Amanda Bauer had feelings for him, deep ones. Just as he did for her.

Reese was no fool, however. So he said nothing, merely nodded slowly, as if agreeing to her command.

The bedside clock glowed red, catching his eye as the numbers shifted from 11:59 to 12:00. And suddenly it was a whole new year. A new future had opened up and the mistakes of the past seemed destined to be washed away, with only good things coming toward them.

"Happy New Year, Manda," he whispered, leaning close to brush his lips against hers. "I hope this upcoming year is one neither of us will ever forget."

Her soft lips parted and she kissed him back, sweetly, tenderly. In that kiss she said all the things she would not say out loud—that she wanted more, but was afraid to let herself ask for it.

She'd changed a lot in the two months he'd known her. The hard shell had started to crack, whether she liked it or not. One day, sooner or later, Amanda was going to realize she was capable of a lot more than she gave herself credit for. She was capable of loving, and of being loved.

He only hoped she let him stick around until that day came.

8

Groundhog Day

"HONEY, WHY DON'T YOU just fly to Pittsburgh and see him?"

Amanda averted her eyes, not wanting to hear another lecture from Ginny, their administrative assistant, who stared at her from across her paper-laden desk. The older woman had figured out months ago that Amanda was involved with someone. She had finally gotten her to talk about Reese after the holidays. Probably because Amanda had walked around with a constant frown on her face since she'd arrived home.

As she'd flown back to Chicago on January 2, she'd wondered if it was time to end the affair. The intimate conversation she'd shared with Reese, and the way he'd made such sweet, tender love to her afterward, had convinced her she had to at least call a time-out, if not quit the game altogether.

Damn the man for slipping past her defenses, breaching her outer walls. Somehow, he'd worked his way into her previously brittle heart. That could be the only explanation for why she'd opened up to him the way she never had to anyone else before.

She'd told him such dark, ugly things about herself, it was a wonder he hadn't run screaming into the night.

It wasn't that she minded so much that she cared for him. The problem was, caring for him meant she wanted to be with him, to keep going with this thing that had sprung up between them. And that, she greatly feared, would not be good in the long run...for Reese. Having feelings for the man meant she didn't want to see him hurt. And she especially didn't want to be the one doing the hurting.

But it was inevitable, wasn't it? Just a foregone conclusion? When the going got tough, Amanda hit the skies.

"Would you talk some sense into her?" another voice said.

Jazz had come into the office, wearing a pair of her mechanic's overalls. A smear of grease on her cheek and the sweat on her brow made her hard labor obvious, but didn't diminish her earthy beauty one bit. "I swear to God, Manda, if you don't call the dude, I'm gonna leave a wrench in your aft engine and just let you fall out of the sky and put us all out of your misery."

Amanda rolled her eyes, feeling very much ganged-up on. "I saw him on Martin Luther King day, and I talk to him every few days."

The government holiday had been a busy one, and a weekday. She hadn't been able to take time off for any out-of-town tryst. But she had arranged for a three-hour layover at the Philadelphia airport. Reese had driven all the way there...and spent those three hours doing incredible things to her in the cockpit of her plane.

She thrust away the warm, gooey feeling those memories inspired. "It's not like I've ended it."

"Uh-huh. But you're planning to," Jazz said knowingly. Ginny nodded in agreement. "Definitely."

She glared at both of them. "It was never meant to be serious. My God, we live in two different states."

"And you fly a plane for a living," Jazz retorted. "An air trip from Pittsburgh to Chicago would probably take less time than commuting in from the suburbs on the El every day."

That was crazy talk. Jazz almost made it sound like she thought Amanda could actually *move* to Pittsburgh and live with Reese. Make something permanent out of what was just a holiday fling.

Wouldn't that be nice? Her, Amanda Bauer, the heartbreak queen of Chicago living a couple of blocks away from Reese's perfect, all-American family with a house full of siblings who adored him and would absolutely hate her guts.

I don't think so.

She stood abruptly, silently telling them the conversation was over. Jazz and Ginny exchanged a frustrated look, but they didn't say anything else, knowing her well enough to know she was already mentally halfway out the door.

Glancing at the clock, she said, "It's late. Time for all of us to call it a day, right?" Forcing a laugh, she added, "Wish that stupid groundhog hadn't seen his shadow this morning. I don't know if I can stand another six weeks of winter."

Jazz muttered something under her breath. Something that sounded like ice-queen, but Amanda ignored her.

Ginny, a little less blunt, walked over and put her hand

on Amanda's shoulder, squeezing lightly. "We love you, honey. We just want you to be happy."

Love. Happy. Two words that hadn't even been in her vocabulary for the first eighteen years of her life. One of them still wasn't.

Not true. Not entirely, anyway. She did love. She loved Jazz and Ginny and her uncle Frank. She loved her sister, if in a somewhat pitying way. She supposed she even loved her parents, because for all their inattention and coldness, they were still her mother and father, after all.

How crazy was it to imagine she might widen that circle and actually let herself love a man? One man?

Maybe it bore consideration.

"I know," she finally replied, giving Ginny a brief hug. Normally not demonstrative, she knew the impulsive act had probably taken the older woman by surprise. Jazz's wide eyes said she felt the same.

"I'll see you guys tomorrow."

Grabbing her keys and her bag, she left them and walked through the quiet office wing of the airport where Clear-Blue Air was housed. As always, it took a while to make her way to the car, and even longer to drive to the city and park in the garage by her building. The entire time, she tried to pull her thoughts into order, to focus and make sense of everything that was going on and how she felt about it.

Feelings and all that stuff so weren't her thing. She just didn't know what to *do* with them.

"Hell," she muttered as she got out of her car, stepping into the frigid Chicago night. It was very dark out, and even inside the parking garage, the wind whipped wildly off the nearby lake. Its gusts made eerie whistles through the openings of the structure, making her freeze for a second before locking up and heading toward the elevator.

As she punched the button and waited for it, an unnerving sensation began on the back of her neck. She glanced side to side, then turned to look behind her. Nobody was around, not a single car moving. She'd gotten home after most commuters but before the club crowd started hitting downtown.

"Okay, cool it," she told herself, knowing she was imagining things. Still, she didn't drop her key chain into her bag, keeping it in her hand with long, sharp keys protruding between her fingers. Just in case.

The elevator arrived and she quickly scanned it to make sure it was empty before stepping inside. She remained close to the control panel, ready to jab the "open" button if somebody she didn't like the look of suddenly came out of nowhere and joined her. But nothing happened, not a sound, not a soul.

She breathed a sigh of relief, laughing at her own foolishness as the doors began to slide closed.

That's when she saw him. A man stood a few yards away, not far from her own car. Fully visible beneath an overhead light, he must have intentionally moved toward it because he had not been there a few seconds ago.

She caught a good look at his face right before her door shut, blocking the view. That glimpse was enough to capture a few quick impressions. Short, compact body clothed in black. Longish, stringy blond hair. Dark-eyed glare.

And suddenly, she remembered him.

"No way," she muttered, her hand tightening on the keys.

But she knew it was true. She'd just seen the thief, the guy who'd mown her down back in Las Vegas.

"You rotten bastard," she added, wishing the door hadn't closed before she'd identified him. Because her first impulse was to go after him and punch his lights out for shoving her into the street.

Then, of course, the wiser head that had kept Reese from doing that very same thing back in Vegas whispered wisdom in her brain. He could be armed, and he'd already proven himself dangerous.

Within seconds, the door reopened on the ground level of the garage. There was no way he could have beaten her here, not unless he'd sprouted wings and flown. He'd been far away from the stairs and the other elevator was clear on the opposite side of the deck. So she wasn't nervous as she stepped outside. Merely very curious. And worried.

"What are you doing here?" she whispered.

It couldn't possibly be a coincidence. The guy had tracked her down, come all the way to Chicago for some reason. But instead of confronting her, he'd played a sneaky game of hide-and-seek, trying to scare her.

But why?

Right outside the garage, people passed by, a nearby bar already swelling with regulars. She put her keys away, though she kept very focused, constantly looking around as she walked the few yards to her building. The doorman offered her a pleasant nod, and once she was inside, she breathed a small sigh of relief.

Not that she was truly frightened. Creeped out, that was a much better way to put it.

"Thanks, Bud," she said to the doorman as she headed toward the elevator. Before she'd reached it, however, she heard a distinct ring. Her cell phone. Grabbing it, she answered with a distracted, "Hello?"

"Is this Amanda Bauer?"

The voice was unfamiliar and throaty, as if the person were trying to disguise it. "Yes, who is this?"

"Long time, no see. You look a little different without the wig."

It was him. The guy from Vegas…the one from the garage. Tense, she stepped into a corner, not wanting to be distracted by the voices of people coming in behind her. "What do you want?"

"I want what's mine. That night when I bumped into you, I dropped a bag of my stuff. The police report says they didn't recover it, which means only one thing. *You* kept it."

"Bullshit," she said with a snort.

He hesitated, as if surprised she wasn't quivering with fright. Which only made her more convinced he was nothing to be afraid of. If he'd had any kind of a weapon, and had the guts to use it, he would have grabbed her in the parking deck and forced her to take him to his so-called loot.

"I'm calling the cops."

She could almost hear his sneer. "What are you going to tell them? That the guy you stole the jewelry from is after you?"

"Oh, I stole your merchandise, huh?"

"Yeah, you did. And I want it. More important, the people I work for want it."

People he worked for? What was there some ring of thieves in Vegas led by a modern-day Fagin and the Artful Dodger? Ludicrous.

"Look, you're crazy. I don't have any jewelry and

you've just wasted a trip to Chicago," she said, feeling more annoyed than fearful. "Maybe you should go back and check all the storm drains or something. It probably fell down one when you tried to kill me."

"Drama queen."

"Psycho asshole."

He hesitated, as if at last realizing he wasn't scaring her one little bit. "Then your boyfriend has it."

She stiffened, suddenly wary. If he'd tracked her down, he might have done the same thing with Reese. "No, he doesn't."

Her tone must have betrayed her tension, because Mr. Robber's voice got a tad more confident. "Oh, he has it, all right. I think I'll have to make a trip to Pittsburgh now."

Damn it. "How did find out who we are?"

"You're famous, lady, don't you know that?"

She had no idea what he was talking about.

"Plus, the people I work for have a few friends in the LVPD. Your names and contact information were right on the police report."

That didn't exactly inspire confidence in the Las Vegas Police Department. She suddenly had the urge to call Parker and tell him to stop worrying about his wife's footwear and start looking for dirty cops.

"I guess I'll be seeing ya," he muttered with a laugh.

"Wait, he doesn't have them, I swear to…"

But she was talking to dead air. The creep had hung up on her.

She quickly flipped back to her caller ID, not surprised that the last incoming call had been from an unavailable number.

Nine-one-one? Officer Parker? Who to call first?

Of course, the answer was neither of those. Without hesitation, she thumbed to her address book, highlighting Reese's contact information on the tiny screen.

She started with his cell number. "Come on," she said when it rang and rang. When his voice mail came on, she didn't bother leaving a message, just moved on to the next one on the list, his house. Again, she got the same result.

"Damn it, where are you?"

The elevator had come and gone a couple of times, and it returned again with a loud ding, letting off a couple who lived on her floor. She smiled impersonally, bringing the phone up to her face to avoid any conversation.

The elevator door remained open and she stared at it. She was in the lobby of her own building, a few floors down from her apartment. But she suddenly found herself unable to walk through the open door and take the short ride upstairs.

An entire evening of trying to track Reese down, to warn him about the crazy thug from Vegas, sounded unbearable. And Jazz's claim about how quick the commute was between Chicago and Pittsburgh kept repeating itself in her head.

She gave it about ten seconds' thought. Then she turned and strode toward the exit. "Bud, would you flag me a cab?" she asked, knowing she couldn't go back for her own car. El Creepo could still be lurking around, and she didn't want him knowing she was heading to the airport, going to warn Reese.

"Sure, Ms. Bauer," the doorman said.

A few minutes later, as she got into the taxi, Amanda

had to smile. Because, as usual, when in crisis mode, she was taking off, hitting the skies. This time, though, instead of running away, she intended to fly *toward* the very person who'd been filling her head with confusion and her heart with turmoil.

Trouble could be heading Reese's way. But she fully intended to get to him first.

WHEN SOMEONE knocked on his front door at ten o'clock that night, Reese immediately tensed. The reaction was instinctive. Even now, two years later, the ring of a phone awakening him out of a sound sleep, or an unexpected knock on the door this late brought him back to the moment when his whole world had changed.

He'd been the one who'd answered the door when the uniformed police officer had come to inform his mother of his dad's accident.

He thrust the dark thoughts away. His family was just fine. He'd left them a half hour ago, happily eating birthday cake at Aunt Jean's mansion, where they'd been celebrating her seventy-whatever'th birthday. Nobody was entirely sure how old she was since she'd lied about the number for so many years.

The only other person he truly cared about was Amanda, and nobody even knew they had any connection. So it wasn't like anybody would be coming to him if something had happened to her.

Besides, he had no doubt she was just fine. Right about now, she was probably in her bedroom, wearing something plain but incredibly sexy, staring at the phone. She would likely be having a mental debate about whether to call and entice him into some serious phone sex, or to continue to try to be strong and resist him, showing them both she didn't *really* need him…at least until she just couldn't help herself.

God, the woman drove him crazy. In a good way, as well as a bad one. And oh, how he adored her for it.

The doorbell rang, then rang again, as if his visitor had become impatient. He forced himself to relax and headed over to answer it, reminding himself not to worry. Still, he couldn't deny his pulse sped up when he turned the knob and pulled the door open.

Seeing who stood there, he jerked in surprise. "What are *you* doing here?"

His four sisters, his brother, his mother, his young niece and nephew and his great-aunt all pushed their way into his house, babbling a mile a minute, all talking over one another.

Reese froze, trying to make his brain process what was happening.

A gaggle of insane people had just turned his quiet respite into a loony bin. Ralph, smart dog that he was, got the hell out, dashing toward the laundry room, probably to snuggle between the dryer and the wall, his favorite hiding spot when he'd done something bad.

"My God, Reese, how could you be so damned irresponsible? How am I supposed to raise my kids to make good choices when their uncle does something so incredibly *brainless?*"

"Reese, are you okay? I'm so sorry if you felt you couldn't share this with us."

"Oh, I've failed you. What would your father say? How could you do such a thing? Where did I go wrong?"

"Were you ever going to tell us, you sneak? I can't wait to meet her."

"Man, wait'll I tell the guys. They're gonna shit bricks."

"How could you! I'll never be able to show my face at school again!"

"When I said to have an adventure, dear boy, I didn't know you'd take it quite *that* far."

All the voices swelled, a chorus of them, but one comment, his sister Debra's, pierced through the cloud of confusion.

"Wait. *Her* who?" he asked, staring at his second-to-youngest sister.

"Reese, are you listening to me?" his mother asked, waving a hand in front of herself, as if to fan away a hot flash. She was red-cheeked, and appeared a bit woozy, although that could have been from the brandy Aunt Jean had been shoving down her throat before Reese's departure.

"Do go sit down before you faint," said Aunt Jean, pushing his mother toward Reese's leather couch. "Molly, take the little ones into the kitchen and get them a snack. They weren't happy that they didn't get to finish their cake."

The sixteen-year-old cast a furious glare at everyone, then grabbed Reese's young niece and nephew and marched them toward the kitchen.

"Jack, why don't you go find Ralph. I'm sure he's scared to death at all of us barging in like this," Aunt Jean said.

Jack frowned darkly. "I'm not a kid."

"No, you're not, which is why you are mature enough to recognize that a poor animal is hiding and frightened in the other room and you should go help him," Aunt Jean said.

Jack had always been a sucker for animals, and he really loved Ralph. Sometimes he came by just to play with the dog, throwing a stick for him, bringing a toy. So the quiet request worked like nothing else would have.

Finally, when it was just the older females of his family, and him, the lone man—Lord, talk about painful torture: estrogen poisoning—Reese repeated his question. "Which *her* are you talking about? What the hell is going on here?"

"Don't act all innocent. The truth is out. Oh-ho, is it out, in a major way," said Tess, the oldest of his siblings. She was the mother of the two kids who were probably right now whining that they had to make do with dry crackers because Uncle Reese didn't have any cookies or good snacks in his pantry.

Seeing Reese's open laptop on the coffee table, since he'd been checking his e-mails before bed, hoping for one from Amanda, Tess grabbed it and began punching letters on the keyboard. "Talk about irresponsible. And stupid!" she snapped, as always, voicing her opinion and not caring how anyone else felt about it.

"Will someone *please* talk to me?"

His mother sniffed, then waved a hand toward the computer screen. Reese turned his attention toward it, wondering why in the name of God everyone was so worked up about a YouTube video.

Then the video started.

"Hey, sweet thing, how late you working tonight?" a male voice said from off camera.

The voice was unfamiliar, but the words rang a bell, though he couldn't place them right away. Nor could he make much out in the dark, grainy image.

Then the focus kicked in, the picture brightened

and cleared. And another voice said, "Got a business card?"

"Sorry, guys, she's retired."

That voice he recognized. "Oh, hell," he muttered, unable to believe it, but knowing what he was looking at. Especially now, as the image got nice and sharp and the screen filled with an easily identifiable couple.

Him. And "Mandy" the hooker. In all her wicked glory.

He glanced away, scrambling to remember everything they'd said and done, wondering if the sly videographer had caught the sexy kiss. Or, worse, the line about...

"...I roped myself a man tonight at that wedding chapel over there. Jeez, what's a girl gotta do to enjoy her wedding night?"

He leaned back in his seat, dropping his head onto the back of the couch and staring up at the ceiling.

This couldn't be happening. It just couldn't.

"You're married?" his mother cried. "How could you get married and not tell us?"

"Worse, how could you marry a poor, down-on-her-luck prostitute? Do you know anything about her? Where is she? Did you abandon her?" asked Bonnie, his twenty-four-year old sister, who shared the middle-child title with Debra but was extremely empathetic and had never seen a tree she didn't want to hug.

"Look," he said, not even sure what he was going to say. "It's not what you think."

"Then what is it?" Tess asked. "Did you or did you not either go temporarily insane or get roofied, and marry some trashy Vegas whore?"

That made him sit straight up and snap, "Watch your mouth." He cast his sister a stare so heated she actually drew back a little. Her mouth remained shut, her lips compressing tightly.

Beside her, watching like the proverbial cat that swallowed the canary, was his aunt Jean. Her mouth was tightly shut, too, only it wasn't because she was trying to control her anger. The wicked old woman was instead trying desperately not to laugh. It was a wonder she didn't hyperventilate from lack of oxygen as she held her breath, trying to contain her merriment.

She was loving every minute of this. Probably taking full credit for pushing Reese completely over the edge.

"I'm just *thrilled* that you're so happy," he said, his voice dripping sarcasm.

She sucked her bottom lip in her mouth, then finally let out a whoosh of air. Rushing toward the kitchen, she said, "I think I'll go check on Molly and the children."

Well, that was one for the record books, a red-letter moment. The ballsiest woman he knew had cut and run. Add that to the rest of this funfest and this might just go down as the strangest night of his decade.

"So tell us, brother dear, what's the story?" asked Debra as she leaned back in a chair and lifted her feet onto the coffee table. She looked to be enjoying this almost as much as Aunt Jean had, but she didn't race for the kitchen in an effort to hide it. "When do we get to meet our new sister-in-law?"

He didn't reply. Instead he stared again toward the computer screen. The video had ended, but he wasn't focused on that, anyway. No, what had drawn his eye was the small counter that indicated how many people had viewed it.

Thousands. Many of whom had left five-star reviews and salacious comments.

He could only shake his head in disbelief.

"Well?" prompted his mother. "Don't you have anything to say for yourself? Not a single explanation?"

Hmm. Which would be worse? Letting his family believe he'd married a hooker during a wild night of partying in Vegas? Or admitting that, for months, he'd been traveling all over the country to play naughty, sexy role-playing games with a woman he was falling head over heels for?

He wasn't sure what he was going to say. Truth or consequences? Either way, he came out looking like a total jackass.

Before he could figure it out, he was, quite literally, saved by the bell. The *ding-dong* was the perfect sound effect for the insane situation in which he'd found himself.

"Good heavens, who can that be?" asked his mother.

"Not a clue," he replied, hearing an almost cheerful note in his own voice.

"Who on earth would simply show up here unannounced at this time of night?" she added.

"Can't imagine. Rude, isn't it?" he muttered, certain the sarcasm would go over her head.

Reese didn't know who had landed on his doorstep this time. He only knew he was grateful to the bastard for giving him an excuse to get up and walk away from the inquisition.

Maybe he'd get lucky and it would be a fireman saying the whole neighborhood had to be evacuated due to a gas leak. Maybe he'd get even luckier and just blow up with it. Anything to escape having to share embarrassing fiction or even *more* embarrassing truth with his nosy, incredibly obnoxious family was a-okay with him.

Whatever he'd been imagining, though, it didn't even come close to reality. He thought he'd been surprised to find his family barging in twenty minutes ago? Hell, that was nothing compared to the shock he got when he opened the door.

Of all the times he'd imagined Amanda Bauer coming to his home, being part of his real world, it sure hadn't been under circumstances like these. Yet there she was, staring at him with uncertainty in her eyes and apologies on her beautiful lips.

"Reese, I'm sorry to just show up like this, but I need to see you and it's not just to jump your bones, even though that's exactly what I'd like to..." Her words trailed off as she looked past him into the house, obviously seeing a bunch of wide-eyed, openmouthed females who'd heard her every word. Her babbling nervousness segued into a momentary horrified silence.

Gee. The night just got better and better.

"Oh, man, *please* tell me you're having a late-night Pampered Chef party, and that's *not* your entire family sitting over there," she said in a shaky whisper.

"'Fraid I can't do that." He forced a humorless smile, stepped back and extended an arm to beckon her in. "Welcome to the asylum."

To give her credit, she didn't run. A few months ago she probably would have. But tonight, she took one tentative step inside, and then another, her curious stare traveling back and forth between him and the women watching wide-eyed from a few feet away.

The silence lengthened, grew almost deafening,

and finally, the sheer ludicrousness of the whole situation washed over him. This was like something out of a movie—a romantic comedy where the hapless hero went from one humiliating situation to a worse one, constantly looking like an idiot in front of the smart, witty heroine.

Fortunately, this smart, witty heroine had a couple of skills that could come in really handy right now. First, she wasn't the type to pass judgment. Second, she was really good at adapting to new situations, as evidenced by her aptitude at role-playing. And finally, she had one hell of a sense of humor. So, with laughter building in the back of his throat, he squeezed Amanda's hand and drew her toward the others.

He opened his mouth to make a simple introduction, trusting that she looked different enough from the woman in the video to be unrecognizable.

He should have known better. Eagle-eyed Tess leaped out of her seat, hissing, "She's the one—it's her!"

Amanda flinched, obviously having no clue what the other woman was talking about. Reese kept a strong, comforting arm on her shoulder. And then, though he didn't really plan to say the words until they left his mouth, he introduced her to the judgmental women watching them with expressions ranging from pure curiosity to horror.

"Amanda, this is my family." He draped an arm across her shoulder and tugged her against him. "Campbell family, meet the little woman."

9

TEN HOURS LATER, the shock of the previous night still hadn't sunk in. Amanda felt dazed whenever she thought about it.

"I just can't believe you did that. Your family must hate me," she said as she walked into Reese's bathroom the next morning. She'd spent the night, of course, having nowhere else to go and not a single piece of luggage.

She now wore one of his T-shirts, which barely skimmed her thighs. Not that she'd needed anything to wear last night. Oh, no, he'd kept her quite warm while making love to her until just a few hours ago, when they'd finally fallen into an exhausted sleep.

She liked the feel of the shirt, liked that his smell clung to it, and she felt perfectly comfortable intruding on him in the bathroom, hopping up to sit on the counter,

Strange that they were already so comfortable with each other, like longtime lovers. Strange, but nice.

"Don't worry about it," Reese said, glancing at her in the mirror. He stood over the sink, shaving, amusement warring with lazy sexual satisfaction in his eyes. "I'll tell them the truth and they'll fall all over themselves apologizing."

The truth? That she was his holiday mistress who'd had him play-acting all across America since Halloween? Oh, lovely.

"But you told them I was your wife."

"No, they told *me* you were my wife and waved their 'evidence' in front of my face to prove it."

The damned video. She still couldn't believe it. Someone had been videotaping them that night, possibly with a cell phone, and they'd never even realized it. Heaven help her if any of their corporate clients stumbled over the clip.

At least she hadn't been *too* easily recognizable. Unlike Reese, who'd been completely uncostumed.

"But you confirmed it. My God, Reese, what were you thinking?"

"Well, I was thinking that my family is composed of a bunch of nosy busybodies and they deserved a little payback." Grinning, he swiped his razor along one more strip of lean jaw. "If my aunt Jean hadn't ducked out the back door before you arrived, I would have seriously considered dropping a pregnancy bombshell, too."

"Whoa, big boy," she said, knowing she sounded horrified. She leaped off the counter and backed out of the bathroom, both hands up in a visible "stop" sign. "That's not even funny."

He didn't look over, that half smile still playing on his mouth as he shaved around it. Ignoring her dismay, he said, "You didn't meet my aunt Jean."

No, she hadn't. Nor did she think she wanted to. She'd met quite enough of the clan last night and didn't care to expand on, or to repeat, the experience.

She slowly shook her head. "I should have denied it."

"I'm glad you didn't."

He could laugh. He wasn't the one being mentally murdered by a group of women who thought she'd either trapped or drugged their brother and son.

Yeah. Denial would have been the way to go. But she'd been so surprised by Reese's claim, she could only watch in silence as his shocked family quietly rose and headed for the door. She'd said nothing when they'd murmured their apologies to Reese for the intrusion and left the house, giving her looks that ranged from disgust to pity. They'd been gone within five minutes of her arrival.

Something else she could have done—followed them out. It would have been even better to have just stayed home in Chicago and kept trying to call Reese all night long rather than flying off to play superhero and protect him from the bad guy.

Superhero my ass. She'd come in person because she'd wanted to see him. That was all there was to it. Excuses about Vegas thugs be damned.

She'd stayed for the same reason. Stayed despite the crazy lie, despite the sheer misery it had been to come face-to-face with the women in his family, playing the girlfriend—no, *wife*—role as if she had some actual right to it. Stayed after facing down the women who all thought she had sex for money.

She felt like throwing up.

Backing up, she stopped only when her legs hit the edge of his enormous bed, then slowly sat down on it. What the hell had she gotten herself into? And she wasn't even referring to the fact that an angry robber had followed her halfway across the country and could be parked outside Reese's door right now, just waiting to break in.

Not that Reese seemed to care. In fact, when she'd told him what had driven her here last night, he'd spent about five minutes being utterly enraged and the next thirty muttering all the ways he intended to punish the guy if he actually had the nerve to show up.

She'd just wanted to call the police. Which was exactly what they were going to do in a couple of hours, once they'd made up the time difference in Vegas and had a good chance of catching Officer Parker on the job.

In the meantime, she didn't quite know what to do with herself. She'd already called Ginny and had her rearrange her schedule. Fortunately, the week looked pretty light and Uncle Frank was able to pick up today's trip. A part-time pilot they contracted with when they were extra busy was on for tomorrow.

Not that she intended to spend another night here. Uh-uh. She had no clothes, and she was already itching to get back to her real life, away from Reese's admittedly beautiful house and ultranormal one.

She wasn't ready to play the role of domestic goddess, or even live-in girlfriend. No matter how nice it had been to wake up in his bed this morning and watch *him* sleep for a change.

Time to run, girlfriend.

But she couldn't leave just yet. Not until they'd reached Officer Parker and found out what he wanted them to do about their unwelcome stalker. They might need to get in touch with the local police. Or she might have to go right back and report to the Chicago ones. She just didn't know.

"Forget it," Reese said, watching her from the doorway of the bathroom. He wore a white towel slung around his lean hips and looked so utterly delicious she wished she'd said yes when he'd offered to share his shower.

"Forget what?"

"You're not going home, not until we've dealt with this guy."

"So, what, I'm supposed to just move in here?"

He shrugged, a non-answer, but the quirk of his lips said he didn't mind the idea.

She forced away the flash of pleasure that gave her, knowing she couldn't let herself be distracted by the realization that Reese really wanted her to stay. "I don't have any clothes."

"It's not the Magnificent Mile, but we do have stores here in Pennsylvania."

She ran a hand through her hair, which she hadn't even brushed yet this morning. "I have a job."

"Your plane's sitting at the airport, isn't it? Who's to say you can't fly from here to go pick up your passengers?"

That was a good point, and was, in fact, exactly what she would have done if she hadn't been able to get coverage for today and tomorrow. But she wasn't ready to give up. "I really shouldn't."

"Yeah. You really should."

The sexy, cajoling smile widened and he walked toward her. She swallowed as that hard, muscular form stopped in front of her, and she couldn't resist reaching out to rub her fingertip along the rippling muscles of his stomach.

"What's more, you really want to," he whispered, stroking her hair and then her cheek.

Amanda leaned closer, wanting to taste that hot skin. She pressed her mouth to the hollow right below his hip, which was uncovered by the low-slung towel. "How will I spend my time?" she asked, brushing her lips across him, toward the long, thin trail of dark hair that led from his flat stomach down into the white terry cloth.

The fabric began to bulge toward her as he hardened right before her eyes.

"Mmm."

He lifted his other hand and twined those fingers in her hair as well, but he didn't guide her closer, didn't force her anywhere she didn't want to go.

She was capable of deciding that all on her own.

A quick flick of her fingers and the towel fell to the floor. His rock-hard erection jutted toward her, and she blew on it lightly, hearing him hiss in response.

She knew what he liked, knew how to please him. But she also knew how to draw out the pleasure. So instead of opening her mouth and sucking him in, she continued to press those featherlight kisses on his groin, letting her cheek brush against his shaft, knowing every soft caress sent his tension—his want—skyrocketing.

"Manda…" he muttered, already sounding near the edge of control.

She moved her hand, sliding it across his strong thigh, one goal in sight. When she cupped the delicate sacs in her palm, handling them carefully, Reese jerked toward her. Only then did she open her mouth and lick at the broad tip of his cock.

"More?" she asked.

His hands tangled a little more in her hair, but he still didn't take what he wanted, merely accepting what she chose to give him.

And what she chose to give him was the pleasure of sinking that throbbing maleness into her mouth. She took as much of him as she could, then tilted her head to take a little more. Using her tongue and soft, gentle suction, plus the careful strokes of her hand between his legs, she soon had him groaning in pure sexual pleasure.

She was ready to go all the way, loving the taste of him and the power of knowing how much he loved what she was doing. But he suddenly pulled back, gently pushing her off him. Then he lifted her under the arms and tossed her back onto the bed, following her down.

He didn't say a single word, didn't kiss her, or stroke her, seeming beyond all capacity to do anything except have her.

It didn't matter. Because when he plunged into her, she was creamy-wet, completely ready for him.

She arched up, taking everything, meeting him thrust for thrust, not even minding that he began to reach his climax long before she was ready for him to. Especially not when he muttered, "I'm sorry. I swear, I'm going to make you come so many times tonight that you won't remember what it feels like not to be having an orgasm."

That sounded like a pretty okay deal to her.

Then he couldn't say anything else, he could only groan as he exploded in a hot rush inside her. Having long since gone on the pill so they wouldn't have to use condoms, she savored every sensation, loving that there was nothing separating skin from skin. Having this man empty himself into her body made her feel connected to him in a way she'd never been with anybody before.

Or maybe it was more than that. Perhaps it was the knowledge that, for the first time in her life, she hadn't just opened her legs to a man.

She had begun to suspect she'd opened her dusty heart to him, as well.

His FAMILY KEPT their distance for the next few days. Reese didn't get a single phone call, not one e-mail, and didn't have to endure any fact-finding trips disguised as casual dropping-by-the-brewery-to-say-hello visits.

That was fine. Just fine. No, he wasn't still furious at them for barging in on him the other night, whether they thought they had the right or not. But he just didn't want to deal with that part of his life right now.

Not when the rest of it was going so very well.

Amanda might not be his wife, she might not even be ready to admit she loved him, but she was sleeping in his bed at night. She was sitting across his table for breakfast each morning, and curling up on the couch to watch a movie with him during the evening. She used his toothpaste and she slept in his undershirts, her shopping trip that first day not including a stop for a nightie.

She'd even done as he'd first suggested and gone back to work from here, flying in and out of Pittsburgh. Her origination point didn't really matter, considering she picked up people all over the country and shuttled them where they wanted to go. So it wasn't a difficult adjustment—he took her to the airport in the morning and picked her up at night.

They were playing a whole new game: normal couple. And he'd never enjoyed anything more.

The only imperfection in the whole thing was that they were playing this game because some sleazy criminal from Vegas might be after her. There hadn't been much progress in the case, though they kept in touch with Officer Parker, a detective from Chicago and a local cop, all of whom were monitoring the situation.

Parker had been furious to learn the thief had been able to access police records to track down the witnesses against him. And their first conversation with him had been quickly followed up by one with someone from the Internal Affairs office.

There was one bit of good news: they'd at least identified the guy. Parker had had a few leads on suspects, and when he found out about the thug's visit to Chicago, he'd narrowed them down even further, focusing on any who had left Vegas. A faxed mug shot later and they'd both identified their man as one Teddy Lebowski, age thirty-six, occupation petty thief and all-around scumbag.

Hearing the criminal was loosely connected with one of the Vegas crime families hadn't made their day. But the fact that he had never been charged with a violent crime, and that Parker considered him little more than a blowhard who didn't have the balls to actually try to hurt anyone, brought a hint of relief.

Sooner or later, the bastard would be caught. Reese half hoped he was stupid enough to show up in Pittsburgh. He'd sincerely like the chance to beat the guy to a pulp for what he'd done to Amanda, both in Vegas and when he'd stalked her in Chicago.

"Hey, you," she said, interrupting his thoughts as he finished locking up his desk for the night. She hadn't had to fly today, and had agreed to come to the brewery for a few hours this afternoon, to see where he worked.

The afternoon had stretched into evening, as a crisis had arisen with one of their distributors. But Amanda hadn't appeared bored, insisting she'd enjoyed touring the place, inspecting the enormous vats and watching the plant workers running the equipment and observing the bottling line.

She'd done a tasting, declaring their amber lager the best, then had sat quietly in a corner while Reese dealt with putting out the fires. Now that the last phone call was done, he stood and wearily rubbed at his temples.

"You look like you could use a massage," she said, rising from the couch that stood against one wall of his office.

"Mmm. You want to play massage therapist now?"

"I think that could be worked into my repertoire," she said flirtatiously.

Arm in arm, they walked outside. A few night workers remained within, but Reese paused to lock up. Then, taking her arm again, they headed for his car.

They hadn't even made it down the outside steps when he saw a familiar vehicle pull into the parking lot.

"Oh, hell."

Beside him, Amanda tensed, going on alert. "What is it?"

"More like *who* is it." The Caddy came to a halt directly in front of them. "You're about to meet my great-aunt Jean."

"Oh, terrific. I can hardly wait for this one," she said, her tone saying exactly the opposite.

He had a lot to say to his great-aunt, both for her leading the charge over to his house the other night—which he had no doubt she did—and for the way she'd slunk out the back door after getting everyone completely stirred up.

The door opened and the elderly woman stepped out of the driver's seat, into the shadows of the parking lot. Then she walked around the luxury auto, approaching them without a hint of wariness, her obnoxious red-leather cowboy boots clicking merrily on the blacktop.

He was about to open his mouth to warn her against saying anything out of line to the woman at his side when Amanda made a small, confused sound. "Mrs. Rush?"

"Hello, Amanda my dear," the old woman said as she reached the steps and walked up them. She leaned over to press a kiss on Amanda's cheek. "I can't tell you how happy I am to see you here." She wagged her drawn-on brows at Reese. "And under such delicious circumstances."

Reese couldn't move, couldn't speak, couldn't put a thought together. He could only stare, wondering how in the name of God his great-aunt knew his lover.

"I don't understand," said Amanda, sounding a little dazed.

But Reese did. Or he was beginning to. "Damn it. You manipulative old…"

His aunt waved aside his anger, as if it were a pesky odor, then lifted her cheek for his kiss.

He didn't give it to her. "You set this up. This whole thing."

"Oh, no, of course I didn't."

"Wait," Amanda said, finally catching on. *"You're* really Reese's great-aunt Jean?"

"Guilty as charged," said the woman.

"Son of a bitch," Amanda muttered, taking the words right out of his mouth.

"Oh, you two, please stop acting as though I had anything at all to do with this fine mess you've gotten yourselves into." She tsked and shook her head, though her lips twitched with merriment. "I merely pushed you in each other's direction. Arranged for your first meeting after I'd planted a few suggestions in Reese's mind—" she turned toward Amanda "—and made sure you were suitably dressed and loosened up for the occasion, thinking you were going to be part of my in-flight costume party."

Her Halloween costume. His last-minute flight. All a setup.

The light dawned. "You called old Mr. Braddock and had him call me to get me to come to Chicago that day."

Her bracelets tinkled as she clapped her hands, as if pleased he'd put it together so quickly. "Yes!" Then she made a cross-my-heart motion and said, "But that was all. Everything else is all on your heads." She almost beamed at them, so wrapped in approval and self-satisfaction she could barely contain herself. "Oh, my, playing such wicked games in Las Vegas." She tapped her fingertip against Reese's chest. "You're a naughty one, Reese Campbell."

He crossed his arms, almost forgiving her, considering she had, in fact, done him one of the biggest favors of his life. But he wasn't quite there yet. "Did you have anything to do with that video clip showing up on YouTube?"

She shook her head hard. "Absolutely not." Then, averting her gaze, she admitted, "Though, I must admit, it was one of my friends whose daughter spotted you in it and sent me a link. I fear that video has gone, what do they call it, viral? You're right smack-dab in the middle of your own fifteen minutes of fame."

Lucky him. And he'd had absolutely no clue. One more reason he wasn't so crazy about the Internet age.

"Let me guess. You just had to show it to the rest of the family after I left the other night."

"Yes. I would say I'm sorry, but you know I'm not."

Of course she wasn't. The woman had never been truly sorry for anything she'd done. Damn, she must have led his great-uncle on a merry chase.

"So, all's well that ends well!"

"No, it's not," he protested. "In case you've forgotten, my family is convinced I'm married to a hooker."

She waved an unconcerned hand. "No, they're not. I straightened that all out."

Almost not sure he wanted to know, he asked, "How?"

"I told them you were flamingly angry and embarrassed that you and Amanda had been caught on camera at a New Year's Eve costume party in Las Vegas. That it was all a joke and you were punishing them for assuming the worst of you."

It wasn't a bad story, come to think of it.

His aunt reached over and pinched Amanda's cheek, apparently not noticing that she'd been almost completely silent. "I knew you'd be perfect for him...and that *he'd* be perfect for *you*. Do forgive an old woman's meddling. It's just that when I see two wounded people who so obviously belong together, I can't stand not doing something about it."

Without waiting for a reply, she turned around and

skipped down the steps like a woman one-third her age. She gave them a cheery wave before getting back into her car and driving away, leaving them staring after her in silence.

He didn't move for a long moment, just stood there absorbing the fact that he'd been completely manipulated by a family member. How much worse must it be for Amanda? God, she barely knew his great-aunt, who, apparently, from what they'd said, was one of her regular customers.

He should have known, should have suspected when his aunt simply insisted he take her place on the private flight to Chicago on Halloween.

"Amanda?" he finally murmured. "Are you all right?"

She hesitated for a moment, then, tilting her head sideways, with her brow furrowed, she replied, "Your family is freaking nuts, you know that, right?"

Startled, relieved, he could only nod and grin. "Yeah."

"I mean, certifiable."

"I repeat…yeah."

She paused again, shaking her head, still staring off down the road where his elderly relative's car had disappeared. When she spoke again, her confusion was gone. So was any hint of anger. "You know, I like that crazy old woman."

"I do, too, when I don't want to strangle her."

"We really have to plan our revenge."

His heart getting lighter by the minute, he nodded in agreement. Plotting together made it sound like she planned to stick around for a while.

Which sounded just about perfect to him.

_10_

AFTER THEY'D LEFT HIS OFFICE, Reese insisted on taking Amanda out for a late dinner. It was after eight, they were both wiped and a steak was the least he could offer her considering she'd just come face-to-face with the person who'd been pulling her strings for months, even though she hadn't known it.

They went to one of his favorite places, not too far from home. It was low-key with good food and great service. There was no play-acting, not even a whisper of suggestion to be anything other than who they were. He didn't mention it, not wanting Amanda to think for a minute that disappointed him.

On the contrary, he couldn't be more pleased that she continued to drop those walls, let down her guard and just be herself...the woman he had fallen in love with.

He knew she didn't want to hear it, and that she'd warned him against it, but there was no hiding the truth, especially not from himself. He'd fallen hard for the woman. Fallen head over heels into the kind of love he had seen in others—like his parents—but hadn't had time to consider he might find for himself.

By the end of the meal, they were laughing as they

tried to outdo each other with extreme revenge plots against Aunt Jean. He had also promised her a dozen times that if and when she met his family again, they were going to be falling over themselves to make up for their assumptions and their coldness toward her.

That would happen even if he had to order, blackmail and browbeat everyone in his family to make absolutely sure of it.

Once they were finished eating, they walked to the car. Night had grown deeper, and she shivered in the frigid air.

"You okay?" he asked, dropping an arm over her shoulder and tugging her closer.

She nodded, clutching her coat tighter around her body. "How can it be colder here than in Chicago?"

"It isn't."

"It sure feels like it."

"I'll warm you up," he offered.

She glanced at him from the corner of her eye. "I'm counting on it."

Once inside the car, Reese watched as Amanda fastened her seat belt, then he put the key in the ignition. But he didn't turn it right away. Instead, he glanced over at his companion, wondering what she was really thinking, wondering if her good mood was covering up any last, lingering resentment over his aunt's confession.

Finally, he just asked. "Are you *sure* you're okay?"

"Uh-huh. I'm about as fine as somebody being chased by a crazy Vegas mobster and mistaken for a prostitute can be." Shaking her head woefully, she added, "It's really not fair that I can be accused of being a hooker and not have the sordid experience to show for it. And called a thief and not have any jewels."

Any final threads of tension evaporated, and Reese had to admire the way she'd taken everything that had come her way in the past several days in stride. Just like she did everything else.

Some women would have left that first night, after she'd been treated so harshly by his pushy family members. Others might have resented being moved around like a pawn on a chess board by a rich old busybody who liked getting her own way.

But Amanda just went with it, laughed and never complained about what she couldn't change. He found that incredibly attractive.

He also really liked the way she teased him about it as they drove back to his place, asking what his sweet old aunt would think if she knew the wild things he'd done to her the night before. As if wanting to remind him, she put her hand on his thigh. Then she began sliding it up, inch by inch.

Suddenly, though, when she went too high, whispering something about making the ride home more enjoyable, he dropped his hand on hers and squeezed, shaking his head in silence.

He didn't have to say anything. She immediately understood. Sucking in an embarrassed breath, she pulled away. "Oh, Reese, I'm sorry."

"It's okay," he murmured, knowing she understood why he was such a careful driver.

There were some games he'd never play, some risks he would never take. No matter what. He'd learned that lesson all too well.

"I'm an idiot." She sighed heavily. "An insensitive twit." She curled up one leg, wrapping her arms around it and resting her chin on her upraised knee, staring pensively out the windshield at the oncoming traffic. With a hint of wistfulness in her tone, she added, "He must have been a wonderful man for you to have turned out to be such a great guy yourself."

"Yes, he was."

He fell silent, not elaborating at first. Talking about his father was probably as difficult for him as talking about hers was for Amanda. Not for the same reasons, of course. Her wounds were old and scarred, and she no longer felt the ache. His were fresh and raw, and he just didn't feel like poking at them and starting the bleeding all over again.

But he could tell by the continued silence that she felt like crap for even suggesting they fool around while he was behind the wheel. The last thing he wanted to do was make her feel worse. So he began to speak.

"His name was Patrick, and he died way too young."

She turned her head to look at him, wide-eyed and tentative. "You don't have to…"

"It's okay. Actually, it's kind of nice to be able to say his name without someone bursting into tears."

She wasn't crying, but he could tell, even in the low lighting of the car, that her eyes were moist.

"He'd worked late, as usual. And he was driving too fast, trying hard to make it to one of Jake's basketball games. He'd missed the last few because of work, and they'd had a big fight about it the day before. He'd promised he'd make the next one. Only…he didn't."

"Oh, God, poor Jake," she whispered, immediately grasping the situation. "That's a lot of weight for a kid to bear."

"Tell me about it. He's been the one I've been most

worried about. He's angry at the world, sometimes mean and rebellious, sometimes still just a lost kid wondering what happened."

Amanda reached across for his hand, this time lacing her fingers through his in a touch that was all about sweetness and consolation. And because she didn't ask any questions, didn't pry at all, just letting him say whatever he wanted, he felt okay about saying it.

He told her about that night. About the nights that followed. About how fucking hard it had been to pick out a casket and decide on a headstone and keep his mother upright and his sisters from sobbing and the business functioning and his brother from blowing his whole life out of guilt, and still maintaining his own sanity amid his own deep, wrenching grief.

It was like someone had pulled a plug on all the words that had gone unsaid for two years. And it wasn't until he'd let them out that he realized just how much he'd needed to say them. Being the strong one, the stoic one, the steady one had also left him the one who'd never been able to release the anger and the heartbreak that had been locked inside him.

By the time he finished, they were sitting in his driveway, and had been for several minutes. They were silent, neither of them even looking at each other, or moving to get out of the car. But finally, once he'd taken a deep breath and realized the world hadn't ended just because he'd admitted to someone else that he sometimes resented his life and his family and even his father, he looked over at her and saw the kind of warmth and kindness Amanda Bauer probably didn't even know she possessed.

"It's all right," she whispered. "Everything you're

feeling is completely understandable." She lifted his hand to her mouth, pressing a soft, gentle kiss on the backs of his fingers. "I'm sorry you and your family had to go through that, Reese. So damn sorry."

"Thank you," he said, rubbing his knuckles against her soft cheek. He opened his mouth to continue, to both thank her and to tell her she needn't feel sorry for him. He also felt an apology rise to his lips, feeling bad for dumping everything on her like that. But before he could say a thing, something caught his eye.

A shadow was moving around the corner of his house.

He stiffened, leaning over to stare past her, out the window, but saw nothing. Thinking about what he'd seen, he knew it hadn't been Ralph. He never left the dog out if he wasn't home. Nor had the shape looked like any other kind of animal.

It had been man-size.

"Stay in the car and lock the doors," he ordered, reaching for the door handle.

"Huh?" She swung her head around to see what he'd been looking at. She figured it out almost immediately. "Is it him? Wait! Don't you dare..."

But he had already stepped out into the cold night, quietly pushing the door closed behind him. Maybe that bastard Lebowski didn't know he'd been spotted.

Reese paused for one second to glance back at Amanda, who watched wide-eyed from inside the car. Making a dialing motion with his hand, he mouthed, "Call 911," then crept across his own front lawn.

Though Parker had said the thief wasn't considered dangerous, Reese wasn't taking any chances. As he passed by the front flower bed, he bent over and grabbed the ugly ceramic gnome one of his sisters had given him as a gag housewarming gift. The thing had weight, it was solid in his palm. And if knocked against somebody's skull, he suspected it would hurt like crazy.

It'd do.

The night was moonless and cold, wind whipping up the few remaining dead leaves still lying in the yard. Reese moved in silence, approaching the corner of the house, carefully peering around it before proceeding.

He spotted Lebowski immediately. The robber was trying to use a credit card to jimmy the lock on the side door leading into the utility room. Muttering curses under his breath, the robber appeared clumsy and not terribly quiet, as if he'd gotten spooked when he'd heard them pull up in the driveway and was now on the verge of panic.

Reese suspected the man had been at it for a while. The fact that the guy hadn't been scared off when he and Amanda had returned said a lot about how desperate Lebowski was to get whatever he thought Reese and Amanda had.

The guy might be sly, but he wasn't much of a criminal. He didn't even notice Reese moving up behind him, jerking in shock when Reese pressed the pointed tip of the gnome's hat against the small of his back. "Make one move and you're dead."

"Aww, shit, man," the guy whined. "No, don't shoot, please don't. I wasn't gonna hurt anybody. I just wanted to get what's owed me and get outta here before you got back!"

"Yeah, so why'd you feel the need to threaten my girlfriend?" he asked, digging the point a little harder into the bastard's back.

"Are you kidding me? I didn't threaten her. The crazy bitch is hard-core, she ain't afraid of nothin'. *She* scares *me!*" The other man risked a quick peek over his shoulder, paling a little more when he saw the obvious rage in Reese's face. "Sorry."

"I most certainly am not hard-core," a voice said, cracking through the cold night as sharp and forceful as a whip.

He was going to kill her. "I asked you to stay in the car." He had to push the words through tightly clenched teeth.

"I did. I called the police, they'll be here any minute. When I saw you had things under control, I thought I'd come back and see if you could use this." She held out her hand, extending the long waist-tie to her overcoat.

Smart thinking. He'd gotten Lebowski to remain still, but hadn't thought ahead to how to keep him that way until the cops came. If the little toad figured out he was being held in place by a ceramic gnome's head, he might not be in the mood to stick around and wait to be arrested.

"Fine. Tie him up."

She moved closer, carefully. "Put your hands behind your back."

"I swear, I just wanted my jewelry. I owe some money to some of my colleagues and if I don't come up with it, they're gonna kill me."

"Well, hopefully they won't be able to get to you in a jail cell," Amanda said, sounding distinctly sour and a little bit pleased at the thought. Not that the guy didn't deserve it.

As she tied Teddy Lebowski's hands behind his back,

yanking the fabric so tight the other man winced, she also said one more thing.

"And you can call me the biggest bitch in the known universe. But I am *not* crazy."

REESE HAD NEVER TOUCHED her more tenderly, more lovingly than he did that night after they'd watched Teddy Lebowski being taken away by the local police. They'd walked upstairs with their arms around each other's waists, her head dropping onto his shoulder in utter weariness.

But once they'd slipped out of their clothes and met in the middle of his bed, sleep had been far from Amanda's mind. And from Reese's.

He'd spent hours stroking her, tasting every inch of her skin, teasing her with soft kisses and slow, deliberate caresses. Every brush of their lips had included a sweet whisper, each embrace a sigh of delight.

Even as he aroused all her senses, bringing her every nerve ending to its highest peak, he'd made her feel... cherished.

Adored.

There had been absolutely no frenzy. They exchanged long, slow kisses that didn't prompt any urgency, didn't make them want to go faster or hurry on to whatever came next. They were delightful just for how good they felt, how intimate and personal and right.

Kissing *was* an incredibly intimate act, she saw that now. She'd always considered it more a prelude to other things, but in Reese's arms, under his rapt attention where every touch brought waves of sensation, she gained a whole new appreciation for a simple kiss.

She'd never experienced anything like it. Never

dreamed that emotional tears would fill her eyes as a man slowly slid into her body. She hadn't ever pictured every slide becoming a declaration and each gentle thrust a promise.

Nor had she ever imagined that when it was nearly over, when she'd lost herself to climax after climax, and had known he was reaching his, too, she'd actually feel her heart split in half at the sound of the words he'd softly whispered in her ear.

I love you.

He'd done it—the unthinkable. The thing she'd warned him not to do. He'd fallen in love with her. And he'd told her so.

Part of her wondered why she hadn't already left, slipping out the minute he'd fallen asleep. The old Amanda would have headed for the hills or the plains or another continent where she didn't have to deal with someone else's feelings that she simply didn't return.

She didn't have to wonder for long. The answer was simple, really. She *did* return them.

And that broke her heart even more.

Lying in Reese's arms after he'd fallen asleep, Amanda couldn't stop thinking about that moment she'd been sitting in the car, when she'd watched him disappear around the corner of the house. She'd heard the expression about your heart going into your throat when terror had you in its grip. But she'd never experienced it...until then.

It didn't matter what Parker had said, or that he'd been right in pegging Lebowski as a cowardly punk who didn't have the nerve to commit real violence. There'd been no way to be sure of that. As the seconds had passed, when her ears had still rung with his sad, grief-stricken whispers about his father, whom he had so loved and lost, she could only imagine the worst.

Losing him, something happening to him…she wouldn't be able to stand it. And though she had no real liking for his family yet, given their behavior the other night and the fact that his mother had looked at her like she was something that had crawled up from out of a toilet, she suddenly felt boatloads of sympathy for them.

The pain of losing someone you deeply loved had to be unimaginable. Which was, perhaps, one reason she'd never wanted to experience the emotion.

Too late. She, the stone-cold, heartbreaking bitch had fallen in love. Completely, totally, irrevocably in love. The ice had melted, her heart had begun beating with renewed energy and purpose. And the man she'd fallen in love with was incredibly sexy, smart, funny, loyal… and great.

Yet, instead of that realization filling her with joy, she could only lie here in the dark and wonder just how long it would be before she screwed it up.

What would be the first callous thing she'd say to start piercing at his feelings for her? What trip would she take, what birthday would she forget, what need would she ignore, what promise would she not keep? How soon before she felt constricted, restrained, and just needed to *go?*

Because those things were inevitable. That was her M.O. No, she'd never gone as far as falling in love before, but it didn't matter, did it? She always let men down, always hurt them, always bailed.

She was just like Uncle Frank. Feckless, reckless, lovable but unreliable Uncle Frank. Everybody said so.

She suddenly wanted to cry. Because how badly did it suck to finally fall in love, *really* in love, and realize you liked the person too much to inflict yourself on him?

Reese was too good, way too good for her. She didn't want him hurt.

Not only that, he had a million and one things on his plate, was obviously at the end of his rope in terms of all the demands placed on him by everyone around him. So how could she add to that, become one more thing for him to worry about, one more weight on his shoulders?

Funny, when he realized she was gone, he would probably think it had something to do with his family, his responsibilities, his ties that bound him so tightly to this place and these people. All the things he'd told her about on the ride home tonight.

In fact, none of that really mattered. She'd told herself she never wanted to be stuck in place, living the same kind of life her parents had lived. But it didn't take a genius to see she didn't have to. She'd been in Reese's house for almost a week, and the world hadn't come to an end. She'd kept going to sleep each night and getting up each day. Kept breathing in, then out. Kept working, kept flying, kept living.

They *could* make this work.

If only she weren't so damned sure it wouldn't last.

It was that certainty that drove her out of bed just after dawn. For a moment, the thought of just leaving, heading for the airport, occurred to her. It had been her standard operating procedure in the past.

But Reese didn't deserve that kind of treatment. Besides, she wasn't that person anymore. Cowardice and immaturity had led her to make those decisions in the past. Now, she wasn't afraid, and she was looking at this through calm, adult eyes.

They couldn't work. Not in the long term. So *he'd* be better off getting out in the short one.

Sitting at his kitchen table, with Ralph—sweet dog, she was going to miss him, too—at her feet, she sipped a cup of coffee and waited for the chill of morning to leave her bones.

It didn't. Not one bit. She just sat there cold and sad, waiting for him to come down.

Finally, he did. When he walked into the kitchen, she could only stare at him. He wore low-riding sweatpants, no shirt, and she gazed at the strong arms that had held her during the night, the rough hands that had brought her so much pleasure. The broad chest against which she'd slept.

God this was hard. Love was hard.

He knew before she said a word that she was leaving.

"Do you need a ride to the airport?" he asked, not meeting her stare.

"Reese…"

He waved off her explanation. "I know. Game's over. Bad guy's caught. It's not even a holiday, so there's no reason for you to stay."

There were a million reasons for her to stay, but one really good one for her to go. All the men in the Dumped by Amanda Bauer group could attest to that. She just wasn't cut out for a serious, loving relationship.

"I did the unthinkable," he added, sounding so tired, and looking so resigned, her heart twisted in her chest. "I fell in love with you when I told you I wouldn't."

He finally met her stare, watching her closely. He

seemed to be looking for something—a sign, a hesitation, a hint that she was happy he loved her.

It took every bit of her strength not to give it to him.

Finally, with a short nod that said he'd gotten the message, he broke the stare. "So, do you need a ride?"

"I can get a cab," she murmured.

"Fine. Goodbye, Amanda."

He didn't say anything else, merely turned and walked back out of the kitchen. His footsteps were hard as he walked up the stairs, and from above, she hard the slamming of the door as he went into the bathroom.

The shower came on. It would undoubtedly be a long one. He didn't have to tell her he hoped she'd be gone when he got out. That was a given.

She followed him up, quickly threw her new clothes in the shopping bags they'd come in. Not really thinking about it, she crossed the room, walking toward the bathroom door. She lifted her fist, half tempted to knock. But her hand unclenched and flattened. She pressed it against the wood, fingers spread, almost able to feel the steam-filled air on the other side of it. Closing her eyes, she leaned her forehead against the door, picturing him in the shower, already hurt by her when it was the very last thing she'd wanted to do.

Better now than later.

Her eyes opened. Her hand dropped. She picked up her bag. Then Amanda Bauer walked out of Reese Campbell's bedroom and out of his life for the last time.

11

Valentine's Day

REESE WISHED THE ONE DAY of the year set aside for lovers took place in March. It would help him out a lot if he could talk Saint Valentine into switching places on the calendar with Saint Patrick, just this once. Maybe Hallmark wouldn't appreciate it, or the flower or chocolate industries, but he could really use an extra month before the big day meant for romance and love—all the stuff he'd had a couple of days ago, before Amanda had walked out of his house.

All the stuff he intended to have again. With her.

It had been hell watching her go. But the minute he'd walked into the kitchen and seen the sad, resigned expression on her face, he'd known she was leaving. He could do nothing but let her, not because of that "If you love something set it free" bullshit, but because he knew her well enough to know there was no point trying to talk her out of it.

As he'd gone upstairs, he'd briefly hoped that seeing how calmly he'd taken it—even though inside he'd been a churning mass of anger, frustration and want—she would realize she was making a mistake and change her mind. Hearing her come up to gather her things, he'd waited in the bathroom, not in the running shower, but standing right on the other side of the closed door. Half wondering if she'd knock. Pretty sure she wouldn't.

She hadn't.

As strong as she was, Amanda wasn't the type to make important decisions on the spur of the moment. She was the retreat-consider-evaluate-then-cautiously-edge-forward type.

He only wished he was able to give her more time to sit in Chicago considering, evaluating, before edging back in his direction. That's why it would have been better if Valentine's Day were a month away. With one month to think about it, he knew—without a doubt—that she'd be calling, e-mailing or showing up on his doorstep.

Maybe not for emotional reasons. Not for commitment and marriage and a lifetime together. It could be just because she *wanted* him, and would send him an invitation to come to D.C. to play a game of senator and naughty aide. Sex. Not love. She was as sexually addicted to him as he was to her, and within thirty days, she'd be jonesing for the kind of hot, wild intimacy the two of them had shared from day one.

So, yeah. She'd call, or write or text.

And he'd go.

It was okay. She could use him to satisfy her deepest needs, because he knew he'd be filled with the same hunger for her. And their game would begin again.

Mainly, however, he'd go because deep down, he knew that one of these days, she was going to finally figure out she loved him, too.

She did love him, of that he had no doubt. Amanda just hadn't acknowledged it yet. Or else she had come up with a million reasons why it couldn't work and had decided not to *let* herself love him.

That was okay, too. He didn't need her to say the words. Sex was enough to intertwine their lives until she was ready, and in a month, she'd be dying for it.

"Curse you for being born in February, St. Valentine," he muttered.

Because while thirty days would have done the trick, five might not be enough. In the short time since she'd left, she might have gotten just a little edgy, but she was stubborn. She could probably hold out longer than that, no matter how incredible the sex between them had been during those nights when she'd slept in his bed.

He had no choice, though. It was February 14, and the romantic in him just couldn't let the day pass without at least giving his best shot at seduction. For the first time in his life, he was in love with the right woman on Valentine's Day. He had to do something about it.

And that was why he was sitting on a plane that was right now landing at O'Hare Airport. He'd booked the best room he could get on such short notice at an exclusive Chicago hotel. Tonight, he would either be there with her, reminding her she'd made the right choice in showing up.

Or he would be sitting in it alone, tossing a box of chocolates into the trash, watching the rose petals strewn all over the bed wilt, and wishing he hadn't wasted a case of champagne by pouring it into the bathtub. Not to mention regretting the oysters he'd already ordered from room service.

He was definitely hoping for option A.

Fortunately, he had an accomplice in his plan to whisk Amanda away for a night of sexy romance. As much as he'd hated to do it, he'd gotten in touch with Aunt Jean and asked her who at Clear-Blue Air would be the best person to ask for inside info on Amanda's schedule. This Ginny woman she'd recommended had been extremely helpful, either because she liked his great-aunt, or she loved her employer. Maybe a combination of both.

From what the woman had said, he had a few hours before Amanda returned to Chicago from her day trip to Cincinnati. A few hours to check into the room, set the scene, then call her and ask her if she had the nerve to see him again this soon.

Asking her probably wouldn't do it. Daring her just might.

All those things churned through his mind as he followed the long stream of passengers off the plane and into the terminal. One more thought occurred to him, too: if this didn't work, he might just have to come back next month and check out the green river and a few Chicago pubs. Amanda would look cute as hell in a leprechaun hat. Or sexy as hell if it was all she was wearing.

Smiling at that thought, he headed not for the taxi stand, but rather toward the offices of Clear-Blue Air. He'd told Ginny he would come by when he arrived, just to touch base and make sure Amanda's schedule hadn't changed. He probably could have called for the information, but he suspected the woman wanted to check him out.

Speaking of calling...*phone*. As he walked, he tugged his cell phone out of his pocket and turned it on. A quick glance at the bars confirmed he had no reception. So maybe Ginny wasn't sneaky and a hopeless romantic, just used to spotty service inside the airport. Though, it could be both.

Making his way through Security, who had his name on the list of authorized visitors to the office wing, he followed the directions Ginny had given him. The airport was huge, he'd always known that. But he'd never imagined the amount of space the public never saw. The hallway seemed to go on for blocks.

Of course the Clear-Blue office was at the end of that hallway. His steps quickened as he realized what time it was. He'd figured this errand would take a few minutes.... It had been thirty since he'd stepped off the plane.

When he was finally within a few feet of the door, he saw it open from the inside. He stepped out of the way to let the person out, not really paying attention. At least, not until a woman emerged. The very woman he did not want to see, at least not until tonight.

"Oh, hell," he muttered as all his plans went up in smoke.

Amanda stared at him, wide-eyed, wide-mouthed, not saying a word. She probably feared he'd turned into some psycho stalker.

"Hey," he said softly, wondering if she'd duck back into the office and avoid him altogether.

Instead, she did something far more shocking. Something that rocked him where he stood.

Without a single word, Amanda dropped the small overnight case she'd been carrying, stepped toward him, threw her arms around his neck and kissed him like she hadn't seen him in at least...a month.

HE WAS HERE. She couldn't believe he was really here, that he'd come to Chicago for her for Valentine's Day.

Kissing Reese, feeling the warmth of his body, inhaling his scent and reliving all the pleasures of his mouth, she found tears rising to her eyes. She loved him, she'd missed him. And she had finally found the man who might give her the freedom to fly when she needed to, but would always be waiting for her when she got back. Or else he'd simply come after her.

Finally, their kiss ended and she smiled up at him. "You came."

"Of course I came." Shaking his head and narrowing his eyes in confusion, he said, "You're supposed to be in Cincinnati."

A quick stab of worry made her ask, "Oh, God. You didn't expect me to be here? You didn't come here to see me?"

He threw back his head and laughed, tightening his arms around her waist. "Crazy woman, of course I came here to see you. But I had this big seduction plan all worked out and you didn't give me as much as an hour to get over to the hotel and set it all up."

"There's a couch in my office," she said, her tone dry. "For you and me, that's about all it would take."

"True." He leaned down and kissed her forehead, murmuring, "But I want to give you more than that."

She sighed, turning her face up so her soft cheek brushed his rough one. "I guess that's okay, then. Ginny's desk *is* right outside my door."

"Hotel it is."

Sounded just fine to her. Anxious to go, to be alone

with him somewhere so she could tell him about all
the wild thoughts that had gone on in her head, and the
wilder feelings that had her ready to burst emotionally,
she slipped out of his arms and bent down to grab her
overnight bag. He took it from her, slinging it over his
shoulder with his own.

She didn't argue—it wasn't much of a burden, because there wasn't much in it. A silky red teddy, a pair
of thigh-high stockings. Just the necessities. Not what
she typically packed for working trips, because she most
definitely had not been on her way to Cincinnati when
she'd run into him. Ha! No wonder Ginny had kept looking at the clock and stalling her with inane questions.
She'd been worried Amanda would fly to Pittsburgh
while Reese was flying here.

"So why aren't you somewhere in or over Ohio?" he
asked as they began walking toward the terminal, his
arm around her waist, their hips and thighs brushing
with every step.

"I had someone else take my flight," she told him.
"Too flipping cold in Ohio."

Even as he laughed at that, given the fact that it had
to be ten-below-cold-as-shit here in Chicago, he jiggled
the overnight bag. "So where *were* you headed?"

There was a hint of amusement in his voice, as if he
knew the answer. Well, of *course* did. He knew she'd
been coming to see him. He hadn't realized it before
he'd arrived here, obviously, but once he'd seen her, once
she'd thrown her arms around him and kissed him with
all the love she felt for the man, how could he not know
she'd want to be with him on *this* of all holidays?

"Where do you think, hotshot?"

"Daytona? It's certainly warmer."

"Not as hot as Pittsburgh."

He stopped when she confirmed it, turning her in his arms so he could kiss her again. This time it wasn't sweet and soft, but deep and hungry, as if he'd been thinking about her since the minute she'd left his house, wanting her all that time.

Or maybe she was projecting how she'd been thinking and feeling. Whatever. All she knew was the man's sweet mouth was covering every millimeter of hers and she never wanted it to end.

Finally, though, because a nearby office door opened and voices intruded, it did.

"Let's get out of here," she whispered, looping her arm through his and leading him back toward the terminal. "I think we have some talking to do."

But not yet. She didn't want to have any deep, important conversation as they walked through the public area of the airport. It was filled with travelers frantic to make their destinations and groaning their way through the long lines at Security.

Since "I'm sorry, I was stupid and I love you" was out, she used the time to fill him in on something a little less personal.

"You're not going to believe the phone call I got this morning." She had intended to tell him about it when she saw him at his place tonight. At least, as long as he let her in the front door.

Not that it would have stopped her if he hadn't. She already knew one of his windows didn't lock right—thank goodness their visitor from Las Vegas hadn't realized it.

"From who?"

"Officer Parker. I guess he was really curious why a sleazy thug would follow us all the way to Chicago, and then Pennsylvania, if he hadn't *really* dropped the jewelry he'd stolen."

Reese eyed her in interest. "Did he have any theories about what happened to it?"

"Yep. Turns out the store owner was apparently just as sleazy. Our friend Teddy *had* dropped his bag of goodies that night—right outside the door of the shop. The owner found it, hid it, then filed a false insurance claim. Parker got him to confess the whole thing."

Reese nodded, appearing as relieved as she had been at the news. "So no more worrying about Mr. Lebowski."

"Correct." Smiling, she added, "Which means you don't have to update your garden gnome for a .357 Magnum."

He chuckled, and a companionable silence again fell between them. It continued as they reached her car and got in it, neither saying much of anything once he'd given her the name of the hotel where they were staying. It was as if he already knew she had a lot to tell him, and didn't want that conversation to start until they were completely alone. She wanted no distractions caused by nosy onlookers, or the need to keep her hands on the wheel.

Besides, a little silence was good. She needed the drive time to put everything into words.

She'd figured she'd have a few hours before arriving on his doorstep in Pittsburgh, armed with a coffee can in one hand, and a teabag in the other. "Coffee, tea or me?" had seemed like a good opening line. Getting him to smile might ensure he didn't slam the door in her face for being such a cowardly bitch and running out on him the other morning without giving him the courtesy of an explanation.

Finally, they arrived at the hotel. She whistled as they walked into the lobby, duly impressed. The man was going all out for this little holiday getaway.

"Don't get too excited," he murmured as they approached the front desk. "I just made the reservation yesterday. They're probably desperate to take advantage of every holiday sucker they can get, so we might end up sleeping in a tiny bed stuck inside a janitor's closet."

She laughed, but honestly didn't care. As long as they could be alone, and a bed was in the vicinity, that was just fine with her.

A few minutes later, when they arrived at their room, she realized Reese needn't have worried. Neither of them were laughing as they walked inside and looked around. Despite the last-minute reservation, the room was beautiful, with a huge, plush bed, elegant furnishings and enormous windows that looked down on bustling Michigan Avenue. She didn't doubt he'd paid several times the rate it would have been on any other night of the year.

"Not bad," he conceded.

"It's amazing," she whispered, not really talking about the room, but about one spot in it.

He had obviously been specific with his requests,

because spread all over that plush, turned-down bed were what looked like hundreds of red rose petals.

"What game are we playing here?" she asked, suddenly a tiny bit cautious and wary.

This looked like wedding-night stuff. And while she'd mentally acknowledged she could not let Reese go without giving the feelings they had for one another a chance, she was in no way ready for rings and white veils.

Liar.

Okay, maybe the thought *had* crossed her mind. But only in a "someday, possibly" kind of way. Definitely not soon.

He accurately read her expression. "Don't worry, if I wanted to play honeymoon, I would have whisked you off to one of those places in the Poconos with the heart-shaped beds and the raised, champagne-glass bathtubs."

She punched him lightly in the arm, instinctively replying, "We are not spending our honeymoon in Pennsylvania!"

Only after the words had left her mouth did she realize what she'd said. And acknowledged the implications.

Seeing the warmth in his eyes, she put a hand up. "Wait. That's not what I meant. I'm not saying…"

"Would you shut up?" he asked, sweetly, tenderly. He lifted a hand to her face, brushing his thumb across her cheek. "Just stop thinking about it, stop talking about it and love me."

It was as simple as that.

She nodded, rising on tiptoe to press her lips against

his. Just as sweetly, just as tenderly. When the kiss ended, she kept her arms around his neck and stared into his handsome face. "I do love you."

"I know."

She kissed him again. "I shouldn't have run out the other day without admitting it."

"I understand why you did."

Her brow furrowing, she lowered her arms and slowly sat down on the edge of the bed, careful not to disturb the flower petals. "You do?"

He pulled a chair closer and sat opposite her, bending over with his elbows on his knees, hands dangling between his parted legs. His expression was serious as he said, "All the difficulties you're sure we have can be dealt with. My family, your family, our jobs, our homes. That whole geography thing they no longer teach in schools."

He didn't have to go on. She had already realized none of those problems really mattered. They could be worked out. In fact, she'd already talked to her uncle about modifying her work schedule so she could, as Jazz had suggested, commute out of Pittsburgh.

Uncle Frank had been incredibly supportive once he'd found out why. Urging her not to let his own bad example lead her to a life as lonely as his, he'd offered to do whatever it took to accommodate her.

"Reese, I…"

"Let me finish, please." The corner of his mouth lifted in a half smile as he completely bared his heart to her.

"I love you. And after we talked the other night in

the car, I realized life is just too damned precarious not to be with the person you love."

She understood. Those very same thoughts had crossed her mind the other morning...only she'd taken the cowardly way out of having to deal with any future pain, loss and heartache. She'd cut and run. Reese was far more daring, willing to risk whatever happened tomorrow for the good things they could have today.

That kind of emotional bravery at least entitled him to the whole truth. "I didn't leave because I was scared for myself, but because I was afraid for you."

"What?"

"I don't want to hurt you, Reese. I love you too much. I've just grown used to the idea that I'm destined to hurt men because I'm not cut out for relationships."

He shook his head. "That's crazy, you wouldn't..."

"I know that now. Sitting at home for the past few nights, going over it in my mind, I realized all those failed relationships I *wasn't* cut out for had one thing in common."

"What's that?"

"They weren't with you."

He pulled her off the bed into his arms, settling her into his lap. Amanda cuddled against him, sucking up his heat and his essence, then said, "How can any loving relationship work if only one person is actually in love?"

"It can't."

"Exactly. And once I realized that, once I acknowledged that I have never been in love with *anyone* until now, I was finally able to let it go. The guilt, the regret, the shame."

He squeezed her. "You have nothing to be ashamed of."

"Tell that to Facebook," she mumbled. But she quickly thrust the thought aside. No room for darkness now, there was only light and happiness, passion and possibility. Love.

"There's nothing wrong with me," she admitted, to both of them. "I just don't fall in love easily."

"Neither do I."

"Which means neither one of us is going to fall out of it easily, right?"

He kissed the top of her head, vowing, "Neither one of us is going to fall out of it at all."

He couldn't know that. No one could know such a thing. But she believed him. With all her heart, with every instinct she owned, she believed him.

"I can't promise not to be insensitive and self-absorbed sometimes," she warned. "Can't say I'll never do something selfish and hurt you."

"Well," he replied after giving it some thought, "I can't say I'll always remember to put the toilet seat down or not squeeze from the middle of the toothpaste tube."

She laughed softly.

He thought about it some more. "I can't promise to let you handcuff me the next time we play cops and robbers…but I might agree to a few silk scarves."

Her laughter deepened, as she knew he'd meant it to. Then Reese got more serious.

"I can't say I'm never going to work late. Or that I won't sometimes just need to be alone with my thoughts. Some days of the year my mood will be dark and I won't want to talk about it."

Hearing that hint of sadness she'd heard in his voice the other night, she understood that. Completely.

"Okay. But I can't promise I'm not going to try to kidnap you away from work once in a while so I can fly us to Aspen to do a little skiing."

He grinned. "That sounds great. Especially because *I* can't promise we won't have one or another of my PMS-ing sisters calling in the middle of the night because she had a fight with her boyfriend and needs a ride."

His family was part of his life. She knew that. The way he cared for them was one thing she loved best about him. Still, the memory of their first meeting intruded. Nibbling her lip, she asked, "Do they all hate me?"

"No! Not one little bit. In fact, two of my sisters showed up at my place last night asking me why I hadn't left yet to come here and win you back."

She breathed a sigh of relief. Though she hadn't wanted to admit it, the idea of a wedding had, indeed, flitted around in her mind once or twice. She'd immediately done her Amanda-thing and started worrying about how she could handle having bridesmaids who hated her guts in her wedding party.

Plus Jazz. Plus her sister, Abby. Oh, Lord.

Not thinking about that now.

"You should also know, my mother called to apologize and asked me to tell you that despite her behavior that first night, she would not be a Monster-In-Law. Which is true—she's sad lately, but she's never been pushy or tried to interfere in my life before. I've been the one hovering."

"That's because you're a good man," she whispered.

A really good, funny, *sexy* man.

A man she deserved.

For the first time, she allowed herself to believe it was possible. She *could* make the right man happy. She *did* deserve him.

Reese was that right man.

Though the rose petals beckoned, and she truly wanted to slip out of her clothes, and get him out of his, so they could express their love in the most elemental, sensual way possible, she had to add one more thing. One more promise, that she intended to keep.

"I won't ever run from you, Reese."

"Sure you will." He smiled tenderly. "But I'll always follow."

* * * * *

Wait! Do you want to know what happened after Reese and Amanda left that hotel room? Well, come back next fall when Leslie Kelly returns to the popular Blaze Encounters *miniseries for*

ANOTHER WILD WEDDING NIGHT

Coming October 2010!

*Rancher Ramsey Westmoreland's temporary cook
is way too attractive for his liking.
Little does he know Chloe Burton came to his ranch
with another agenda entirely....*

That man across the street had to be, without a doubt, the most handsome man she'd ever seen.

Chloe Burton's pulse beat rhythmically as he stopped to talk to another man in front of a feed store. He was tall, dark and every inch of sexy—from his Stetson to the well-worn leather boots on his feet. And from the way his jeans and Western shirt fit his broad muscular shoulders, it was quite obvious he had everything it took to separate the men from the boys. The combination was enough to corrupt any woman's mind and had her weakening even from a distance. Her body felt flushed. It was hot. Unsettled.

Over the past year the only male who had gotten her time and attention had been the e-mail. That was simply pathetic, especially since now she was practically drooling simply at the sight of a man. Even his stance—both hands in his jeans pockets, legs braced apart—was a pose she would carry to her dreams.

And he was smiling, evidently enjoying the conversation being exchanged. He had dimples, incredibly sexy dimples in not one but both cheeks.

"What are you staring at, Clo?"

Chloe nearly jumped. She'd forgotten she had a lunch date. She glanced over the table at her best friend from college, Lucia Conyers.

"Take a look at that man across the street in the blue shirt, Lucia. Will he not be perfect for Denver's first issue of *Simply Irresistible* or what?" Chloe asked with so much excitement she almost couldn't stand it.

She was the owner of *Simply Irresistible,* a magazine for today's up-and-coming woman. Their once-a-year Irresistible Man cover, which highlighted a man the magazine felt deserved the honor, had increased sales enough for Chloe to open a Denver office.

When Lucia didn't say anything but kept staring, Chloe's smile widened. "Well?"

Lucia glanced across the booth at her. "Since you asked, I'll tell you what I see. One of the Westmorelands—Ramsey Westmoreland. And yes, he'd be perfect for the cover, but he won't do it."

Chloe raised a brow. "He'd get paid for his services, of course."

Lucia laughed and shook her head. "Getting paid won't be the issue, Clo—Ramsey is one of the wealthiest sheep ranchers in this part of Colorado. But everyone knows what a private person he is. Trust me—he won't do it."

Chloe couldn't help but smile. The man was the epitome of what she was looking for in a magazine cover and she was determined that whatever it took, he would be it.

"Um, I don't like that look on your face, Chloe. I've seen it before and know exactly what it means."

She watched as Ramsey Westmoreland entered the store with a swagger that made her almost breathless. She *would* be seeing him again.

* * * * *

Look for Silhouette Desire's
HOT WESTMORELAND NIGHTS
by Brenda Jackson,
available March 9 wherever books are sold.

THE WESTMORELANDS

NEW YORK TIMES
bestselling author

BRENDA JACKSON

HOT WESTMORELAND NIGHTS

Ramsey Westmoreland knew better than to lust after the hired help. But Chloe, the new cook, was just so delectable. Though their affair was growing steamier, Chloe's motives became suspicious. And when he learned Chloe was carrying his child this Westmoreland Rancher had to choose between pride or duty.

Available March 2010 wherever books are sold.

Always Powerful, Passionate and Provocative.

SPECIAL EDITION

FROM *USA TODAY* BESTSELLING AUTHOR
CHRISTINE RIMMER

A BRIDE FOR JERICHO BRAVO

Marnie Jones had long ago buried her wild-child
impulses and opted to be "safe," romantically
speaking. But one look at born rebel Jericho Bravo
and she began to wonder if her thrill-seeking side
was about to be revived. Because if ever there was
a man worth taking a chance on, there he was,
right within her grasp....

*Available in March
wherever books are sold.*

HARLEQUIN *Presents*

Two families torn apart by secrets and desire
are about to be reunited in

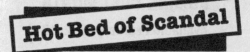

Hot Bed of Scandal

a sexy new duet by

Kelly Hunter

EXPOSED: MISBEHAVING WITH THE MAGNATE

#2905 Available March 2010

Gabriella Alexander returns to the French vineyard she
was banished from after being caught in flagrante with the
owner's son Lucien Duvalier—only to finish what they started!

REVEALED: A PRINCE AND A PREGNANCY

#2913 Available April 2010

Simone Duvalier wants Rafael Alexander and always has, but
they both get more than they bargained for when a night of
passion and a royal revelation rock their world!

www.eHarlequin.com

HP12905

COMING NEXT MONTH

Available February 23, 2010

#525 BLAZING BEDTIME STORIES, VOLUME IV
Bedtime Stories
Kimberly Raye and Samantha Hunter

#526 TOO HOT TO HANDLE
Forbidden Fantasies
Nancy Warren

#527 HIS LITTLE BLACK BOOK
Encounters
Heather MacAllister

#528 LONE STAR LOVER
Stolen from Time
Debbi Rawlins

#529 POSSESSING MORGAN
Bonnie Edwards

#530 KNOWING THE SCORE
Marie Donovan